WHITE STAR

WHITE STAR

A Dog
on the *Titanic*

BY

MARTY CRISP

Holiday House / New York

ACKNOWLEDGMENTS

Special thanks to Walter Lord, who brought the story of the *Titanic* into modern times, and George Behe, who helped me understand it. It was my great pleasure to be received into Lord's New York City home to talk about dogs on the *Titanic*. His apartment was definitely as close to the *Titanic* as a Titaniphile can get on dry land!

Thanks also to my editor, Suzanne Reinoehl, whose patience and avid interest in the subject helped tremendously.

This book also benefited from the expertise given generously by Roy Mengot, Andy Hall, Phillip Gowan, Mimi Lai, and many other helpful Titaniphiles on Jeff Newman's and Mark E. Reynolds' *Titanic* electronic mailing lists.

The publisher would like to thank the Cunard Line, Ltd. and the National Archives
for providing reference materials, including the blueprints
of the White Star Line's S. S. *Titanic*.

Library of Congress Cataloging-in-Publication Data
Crisp, Marty.
White Star : a dog on the Titanic / by Marty Crisp—1st ed.
p. cm.
Summary: Twelve-year-old Sam, a passenger on the Titanic's maiden sea voyage,
volunteers to help care for the dogs in the ocean liner's kennel and becomes fast friends
with the Irish setter of J. Bruce Ismay, the ship's owner.
Includes bibliographical references (p.).
ISBN 0-8234-1598-8
1. Titanic (Steamship)—Juvenile fiction. [1. Titanic (Steamship)—Fiction.
2. Shipwrecks—Fiction. 3. Dogs—Fiction. 4. Survival—Fiction.] I Title.
PZ7.C86942Wj 2004
[Fic]—dc22
2003062551

To my husband, George Byron Crisp,
even though he says, "It sank, get over it."

PROLOGUE

It is surprising how little is known about the dogs of the *Titanic,* but there *were* dogs aboard during that fateful maiden voyage in April 1912. No one knows for sure where the ship's kennel was located or the exact number of dogs on board. Those records went down with the ship. But we do know that a dog show had been scheduled toward the end of the voyage, for Monday afternoon, April 15, 1912. The ship sank that morning.

Dogs feature in some of the *Titanic's* enduring legends. One woman supposedly refused to get into a lifeboat without her Saint Bernard. There is also the story of Rigel, a Newfoundland that reportedly led Lifeboat Number 4 to safety. *Titanic* historians have since disproved that tale.

Two other facts are known about *Titanic's* dogs. First, someone freed the dogs that were locked in the kennel before the ship went down. Second, three dogs actually survived the sinking.

The story of the *Titanic* is full of cowardice and courage, despair and determination. People have been telling tales about the great ship for almost a century now.

This is a story about the dogs—the dogs of the *Titanic.*

CONTENTS

CHAPTER 1

Em-*bark*-ation

Cherbourg, France
Wednesday, April 10, 1912

"Dogs! There really *are* dogs on the *Titanic!*"

Bucky grinned at Sam. "Told you. Why else do you think they call it em-*bark*-ation when a ship sails?"

Sam nodded, his eyes glued to the little transport boats down below. The tenders had brought new passengers across Cherbourg Harbor to board the *Titanic*. A lot of the newcomers had dogs.

Sam had already spotted a bat-eared French bulldog, a hulking Saint Bernard, two yapping Pomeranians, and a panting chow chow.

He leaned far out over the well-deck rail to get a better look. Suddenly the tuppence his gramp had given him for luck slid out of his front jacket pocket. The coin arced through the air.

Sam lunged for it.

"Whoa there!" Bucky grabbed the tail of Sam's jacket. He hauled him in just as a seagull swooped down and caught the coin before it hit the water.

"Drat!" Sam said. "Now that gull has all my luck!"

"He won't enjoy it," Bucky assured him. "He wanted some of that bread the ladies on the boat deck are tossing. Your tuppence will give him a bellyache."

Sam sighed. With or without the tuppence, his luck had been going downhill ever since his mother had married again. Since she remarried while Sam was taking his final exams, he hadn't been allowed to go home for the wedding. His mother was being more cautious with money these days. So he'd never even met his new stepfather. But now his mother wanted Sam to leave England, where he'd been staying with his grandparents, and come to America. So this morning in Southampton, Sam had waved good-bye to his gramp and boarded the *Titanic*. When Sam got to America, his mother said they could all be a family again.

As if it were that easy.

Sam hawked up a wad of spit, the way he'd seen the sailors do it, and aimed at one of the circling gulls. He missed and the spit ran in a gooey glob down his chin. He wiped it off with his sleeve.

Even if he'd lost his lucky coin, he still had Bucky. At

St. Ives, Bucky Kingsbury had taken Sam under his wing when Sam first arrived from America. He slept in the bed next to Sam and must have heard him cry himself to sleep those first nights in England. But he never taunted Sam for it. Bucky's friendship had eased Sam's homesickness. He had been Sam's friend when Sam needed a friend more than he ever had before.

"You were right about the dogs being on board, Buck." Sam turned and they bumped first one elbow and then the other in their secret signal of brotherhood. "You really *do* know everything about this ship!"

"Told you I did. I can tell you the number of watertight compartments, how many tons of coal they loaded for the boilers, and how many lookouts they keep in the crow's nest. Whatever you want to know," Bucky said. "I need to find Mr. Andrews tomorrow and suggest a few improvements."

"Uh-huh." Sam peered over the rail. The tenders appeared to be finished unloading, and the gangways were being hauled in. "*You're* going to tell this ship's engineer how to make the *Titanic* better? He probably doesn't even talk to people who have less than three university degrees. Let alone a kid. Besides, everybody knows this is the best ship ever made."

"*Titanic*'s a great ship, but she could be even better," Bucky said.

Sam rolled his eyes. "All right, genius, if you know everything, tell me where the kennel is. I want to have a look."

"They're up on top, on the boat deck. That's where the pilot house and the wireless room and the gymnasium are. And the lifeboats, of course," Bucky added. "It was supposed to be on F deck, but Andrews moved it at the last minute. It's never too late for improvements, like I said."

"Race you!" Sam ran for the steep stairs that would take them up three decks to the top of the *Titanic*.

"Last one there is a barnacle's bum!" Bucky scrambled to try to pass Sam.

But Sam swung himself up two steps at a time, bending low to block Bucky from squeezing under his arms. Sam would get to the kennel first. When there were dogs to see, you could bet he'd win any race.

Sam and Bucky reached the door, just aft of the third funnel, at the same time. Sam ran in first, almost colliding with a tall, skinny, redheaded boy who didn't look old enough to be a real sailor.

"We came to see the dogs," Bucky announced above a clamor of woofs, yaps, and barks.

"Shut the door!" bellowed the redhead. "Before somebody starts complaining about this racket."

Bucky nodded and pulled the door shut with a clang.

"Are you in charge here?" Sam asked.

The boy gave Sam a mock salute. "That'd be me, Phineas MacDougal. Captain of the Canines. But call me Finn. I'm really only a cabin boy."

Sam and Bucky introduced themselves, and then Sam looked around at the polished teakwood cages, the burlap sacks of feed, the bales of clean straw, and the cast-iron sink with a hose attached to its spigot. The French bulldog was here, the chow chow, one Pomeranian, and two Airedales.

"Where's that silly-looking little white dog we saw come aboard?" Bucky asked.

"Ah, you must mean Frou-Frou, the darling of that newlywed couple, the Bishops. A lot of the dogs stay in their owners' cabins and only come up here when life down below gets too fancy for them."

"How'd you get stuck with this job?" Bucky asked, wrinkling his nose at the musky odor of lots of dogs in one small room. Only a ventilation register near the ceiling let in fresh air.

"Are you kidding?" Sam knelt and scratched under the muzzle of an Airedale. "I think it smells just fine, and this would be a *great* job!" He looked over his shoulder at Finn. "Could you use any help?"

"Aye, lad, if you mean what you say." He handed Sam a long-handled, cupped shovel. "Help yourself."

He tried to hand a second shovel to Bucky, who pushed it aside. "I study ship design," Bucky said, squaring his shoulders. "I *don't* clean up after dogs."

"Suit yourself," Finn said with a shrug. Then he went to work cleaning out a cage. "But next time could you design a ship with doggie toilets we could just flush?"

"My ship," Bucky declared as Sam and Finn worked, "will have everything. Beds that make themselves. Automatic pilots to steer the course. And a giant periscope so nobody has to climb up to be on lookout. *My* ship won't just be unsinkable. It'll be unbelievable!"

"That it will," Finn agreed with a laugh.

"Come on." Bucky tugged on Sam's jacket. "I want to see the wireless room."

Sam rubbed his nose against the wet nose of the tiny Pomeranian, almost small enough to fit through the bars of her cage.

"Let's go, Sam."

"I'll be back early tomorrow, Finn," Sam called as Bucky jerked him out the door.

"I'll be glad to see you. We can . . ." but the rest of Finn's sentence was lost as Bucky let the metal door clang shut behind them.

CHAPTER 2

A Dog Down Below

Queenstown, Ireland
Thursday, April 11, 1912

Sam wished Bucky were out on deck with him to see this, but Bucky was off eating lunch.

Sam didn't need lunch. He *had* to be here to observe the new passengers coming aboard and to write things down. That's why his grandfather had given him the little leather notebook with the gold clasp. Sam's father had been a reporter, and Gramp wanted to see if Sam had reporting in his blood. After writing down everything he saw on the voyage, Sam would send it from America back to his grandparents.

Sam stood in a crowd of people, many of them tradesmen who'd come aboard to sell their wares: delicate lace, woolen scarves, homemade soda bread. Passengers leaned on the rails for a last glimpse of land.

The small tender *Ireland* bobbed on the water directly below him, full of passengers being ferried across Queenstown Harbor. The *Titanic* seemed able to swallow more and more new passengers, without, as Bucky had put it, "even a burp."

Now there was an Irish setter down there on the smaller boat, waiting to cross the rocking gangplank into *Titanic*'s open hatchway. The setter looked so much like his dad's dog, Sam could hardly believe it.

Rusty had had that same burnished red coat and the same patch of white on his chest. But Rusty had once gotten his tail caught under the wheel of their carriage, and, after that, it hung at what his dad called half-mast. This dog's tail waved high and straight.

The setter paused before stepping onto the gangplank and looked up at Sam, his tail wagging faster than it had before. Sam could barely breathe as he stared back at the dog. He half expected to see his father come out and take the dog's lead. But of course, that was impossible.

"Hul-*lo* down there!" Sam called, raising both hands and waving. The dog couldn't have heard him, but when he saw Sam waving, he pranced excitedly from paw to paw and gave a bark.

The setter confidently moved across the rolling gangplank with the crewman holding his leash. Sam chuckled at the crewman's comical struggle to lead the dog on the unsteady plank. The setter finally disappeared into the hatchway. Sam jammed his notebook into his coat pocket, but his pencil was gone. He'd just been using it a second ago. Well, he didn't have time to look for it now.

Sam sprinted down the promenade of the A-deck, dodging around a lady whose tiny Pomeranian poked out of her handbag.

He ducked around a group of ladies haggling with tradesmen, and smacked right into a deck chair.

"Oof!"

He sprawled across a pair of legs.

"Careful there," the owner of the legs said mildly, reaching out a hand to steady Sam. The gentleman wore a bowler hat and puffed on a polished walnut pipe. A delicious-smelling cloud of cherry tobacco smoke hung around him and tickled Sam's nose. Countless times Sam's father had packed his own pipe with that same sweet, crumbly tobacco.

Sam swallowed hard and pushed himself to his feet. The gentleman leaned forward, concern in his eyes.

"You all right, son?"

Sam nodded, feeling a flush of color rising from his neck to his cheeks.

"Big excitement today." The man smiled at Sam.

"Last day in sight of land. Wouldn't want to miss that, would you?"

"Yes sir. No sir. Sorry, sir."

Sam looked down at his feet. There it was!

His pencil!

He forgot he'd put it behind his ear. It must have fallen to the deck when he crashed into the man.

Sam quickly bent to retrieve it and banged his head hard against something. He straightened up, leaving the pencil and rubbing the throbbing spot on his forehead.

"It seems two men can't occupy the same space at the same time." The man in the bowler was rubbing his forehead, too.

"No sir. Sorry, sir."

"Stop calling me sir. You're making me feel a hundred years old." He smiled and stuck out his hand. "I'm Robert Daniel, a banker from Philadelphia, Pennsylvania, and very pleased to meet you."

Sam shook Mr. Daniel's hand.

"I'm Sam Harris, sir."

Mr. Daniel rolled his eyes. "What did I tell you about calling me sir?"

"Oh. Sorry, sir. Mr. Daniel."

Mr. Daniel laughed. "So how old do you *think* I am?"

"Forty?" Sam guessed.

"Twenty-seven," Mr. Daniel shot back. "Maybe I

better shave off this silly mustache if it makes me look *that* old."

"Oh, no sir. You don't look nearly as old as somebody who's *really* old, like . . ." Sam searched his mind for an example. "Like Captain Smith."

Mr. Daniel laughed again. "Well, seeing as how he's got white hair and a white beard, I'm glad I don't look *that* old! So, how old are you, Sam?"

"Twelve. Thirteen in December."

Mr. Daniel nodded solemnly. "Of course. It's April, but still worth borrowing a bit of age from December. You look familiar. You and your friend were watching the dogs loaded yesterday, weren't you?"

Sam nodded. "Yes sir. That was me and Bucky. And there's another new dog just come aboard. An Irish setter."

"Like dogs, do you?" Mr. Daniel handed Sam his pencil. "I'm interested in them, too. You'll have to meet my dog, Sam. He's up in the kennel right now."

Sam inched a step toward the stairs, eager to see the new dog, but Mr. Daniel put a hand on Sam's arm, stopping him.

"That dog you're so keen to see is Mr. J. Bruce Ismay's champion Irish setter. Ismay plans to use the dog for advertising, like that little white terrier in the Victor Talking Machine Company advertisements. The

11

ones that say: 'His master's voice.' That setter isn't just any passenger's dog, Sam. He's a star."

"Yes sir!"

Mr. Daniel winked and let go of Sam's arm. Sam spun on his heel and leaped up the steep stairs to the boat deck on his way to the kennel.

The new dog was waiting for him.

CHAPTER 3

A Star Is Born

Thursday, April 11, 1912

Sam vaulted over the gate separating the first- and second-class promenades on the boat deck. Finn was just coming out of the rear elevator with the Irish setter trotting on a leather lead. He must have gotten the dog from the crewman on the tender.

"Sam!" Finn saluted. "So, what do you think of this beauty?"

"He's the best!" he shouted over the screaming of the seagulls that were scavenging *Titanic*'s newly dumped garbage. Finn opened the kennel door and the barking of dogs drowned out the gulls.

"He looks just like my dad's old dog."

"Does he now?" Finn led the dog inside and the barking got louder. "He's barely a year old. They tell me he's to be the pride of the White Star Line. But he needs a bit of practice at being dignified and properly snobbish first."

The dog gave a yank on his leash and danced about with his front paws, yelping happily.

Sam dropped to his knees and slowly reached out a hand so the dog could sniff it. The dog scrambled closer to him, smothering Sam's cheek with wet kisses.

"What's his name?" Sam asked. The dog rested his head on Sam's shoulder for a few seconds before slurping his ear.

"Don't think he has one yet." Finn filled an empty crate with clean straw from the bales in the corner. "I've just been calling him Dog."

"He has to have a name," Sam protested.

"Gentlemen!" a voice boomed. "I've come to see the famous White Star dog I've heard so much about!" Robert Daniel stood at the kennel door.

He squatted down and ran a practiced hand over the setter's back and head, even as the dog waggled about. He reached for the setter's muzzle and pulled back his lips, revealing white teeth and healthy-looking pink gums. "All I can say is, treat this dog with respect, boys. He's a bit feisty now, but when he's finished his training, he may turn out to be more famous than John

Jacob Astor himself, once Ismay gets his new advertising campaign up and running."

He pointed to the splotch of white fur on the dog's chest and whistled softly. "Any more white than that in his coat, and he'd be no good for the show ring. A bit of white's allowed in the breed standard. But Mr. Ismay found himself a dog with a white patch shaped like a star and still show-ring quality. Made to order, if you ask me."

"White Star's dog," Sam whispered to the dog. Then he turned to Mr. Daniel. "Do you think Mr. Ismay would mind if I just called him Star?"

Mr. Daniel opened the door of one of the crates and scooped up a French bulldog. "It's not whether or not Ismay would mind." He grinned at Sam. "It's what the *dog* likes. Take this fella here." He bounced the little bulldog in his arms, allowing him to lick his nose and mustache. "On paper, he's Gamin de Pycombe, as fancy a name as any dog could put up with. I bought him in France, and he's going to be the start of the finest line of French bulldogs in America. But just between you and me, his friends call him Pye. He seems to like it that way. So ask the dog, Sam. He'll know his proper name when he hears it."

"Star?" Sam whispered to the dog.

15

The red setter rushed at him, knocking him over and nuzzling him with his nose. Sam laughed and tried halfheartedly to fend him off.

"I'd say you've found the perfect name, Sam. Every dog has a secret name that he knows is his own, no matter how many owners call him however many silly things they want. That dog knows he's Star."

As Sam and Star rolled on the kennel floor together, getting straw all over themselves, Sam felt happy for the first time in days. This was the first thing that felt completely right since his father had caught the influenza six years ago. His father had been quarantined, and Sam wasn't allowed to go near him. Rusty had stayed by his father's side, while Sam could only look in at him through a closed window.

Sam could still hear his father's muffled voice through the glass, promising everything would be all right.

It hadn't been. His father's death had been bad enough. But then his mother gave Rusty away. Rusty should have been his. His mother said the dog needed more care than a six-year-old boy could manage.

She might have managed, if she'd tried. But she could barely get out of bed after his father died. She sat and stared out her bedroom window, letting trays of food sit cold and uneaten on her dressing table. Sam's grandmother had moved in with them. She spoon-fed soup to Sam's pale, shadow-eyed mother.

It had been decided that Sam and his mother should go to England to live with his father's parents for a while. The trip had been meant as a short one, a few months abroad that would do them both good. Sam didn't fight it. He'd lain awake too many nights, listening to his mother's sobs.

But his mother didn't go after all. The doctor said she was too weak and sick to withstand an ocean crossing. So she let Gramp come and get him. She hadn't even been able to pack Sam's things. Sam watched his grandfather finish packing what his mother had started. To Sam, it felt like packing memories away in his steamer trunk.

Sam had gone to England as planned, leaving his mother behind. He'd stayed for six years, not six months. Oh, his mother had written. She'd written every week, and Sam had saved the letters. Gramp made him take most of them out of the trunk when he was packing for the trip back to America. Otherwise, Gramp said, there would be no room for clothes. But Sam needed the letters. The letters were more real to him than the woman he would meet in New York. His mother was a stranger. And now she was married to a stranger. His father was gone. Rusty was gone. But Star—Star was here.

"Passing Roche's Point," boomed a voice through a megaphone out on the boat deck.

That was that, then. The last bit of England was behind him. Now there was Star and the ocean and the gentle roll of the *Titanic*. Sam couldn't let himself think any farther ahead than that.

CHAPTER 4

Luck of the Irish Setter
Friday, April 12, 1912

"We're never going to find the ship's cat down here," Bucky whispered. He peeked around the corner of an iron boiler as big as a house. They'd already checked the storage holds, the squash court, and the mail-sorting rooms. Now they were deep in the bowels of the ship.

"You heard the stewardess. The cat has a litter of kittens. She's bound to turn up soon. And if anyone can sniff her out, Star can." Sam gave Star a pat on the head. Star's tail thumped against Sam's leg.

"Let's check out the coal bunkers over there." There was the sound of heavy footsteps.

"Stop right there! You hear me, boys? Just what do you think you're doing down here?" A burly man, his frowning face smudged with coal dust, was trotting after them.

"Run, Sam! Go left, I'll go right. It's every man for himself!" Bucky took off around the iron boiler.

Sam ran down the aisle between rows of steaming, clanking boilers, with Star at his heels.

The stokers, glistening with sweat, stopped shoveling coal and leaned on their shovels, laughing and hooting.

"Go on with you, Scottie," one of them called out. "Move those tree stumps you call legs. The lads are getting away from you."

Sam felt as if his lungs would burst if he ran any faster in the choking heat of the boiler room. He ducked through a bulkhead door, saw a hatch, and dived head-first into a coal bunker. Star followed him with a joyful bark.

Sam grabbed Star's muzzle with both hands and whispered, "Shhh!" Then he pulled the hatch door closed as slowly as he could, trying to keep it from creaking.

"Where are you?" a voice bellowed. "Passengers aren't allowed down here. When I get my hands on you rascals, I'll . . ."

Star's tail tickled Sam's leg. Coal dust was thick in the air, and Sam pinched his nose to keep from sneezing. The mound of coal they sat on had sharp edges that cut into his legs and bottom.

Finally, the hoarse voice of the red-faced stoker faded away.

Sam allowed himself a breath.

Slowly, quietly, he turned, trying not to start an avalanche of coal. Mr. Ismay would doubtless make Sam walk the plank if anything happened to his dog. Sam pushed the hatch cover open, just wide enough to peek outside.

No one was looking his way.

Sam pushed the hatch open wider. He heard muffled voices some distance away; Bucky, arguing with someone.

He and Sam and Star had snuck through at least two doors marked Crew Only just to get down here to the orlop deck, one deck up from the ship's very bottom. Now they had to get back out.

Sam wiggled through the hatch and motioned to Star.

"Come on," he whispered. Star lunged down the aisle toward the other voices, but Sam grabbed his collar. This was his only chance to get the dog back to the kennel without being seen.

He caught a quick glimpse of Bucky talking with two stokers as they worked, trying to show them a better way to shovel coal. Leave it to Bucky to create a distraction.

"Amazing!" Bucky was saying. "How many knots of speed can you get from a single ton?"

The voices faded away under the roaring of the boilers.

"Come on, Star. This way." Sam pulled on the dog's collar, leading him back down a hall where there was a steep set of metal stairs at the end. Star was smart, but he couldn't climb the boiler room ladders.

Sam started up the stairs, pushing Star in front of him. The dog's tail whapped him in the face, but Sam only shoved harder. Once they reached the top, they didn't stop running until they were on the other side of the second door marked Crew Only.

Sam bent over, nursing a cramp in his side, then studied the dog sprawled out in front of him. Star's red fur was so streaked with coal dust, he looked more like a black Lab than an Irish setter.

"You need a bath," Sam said.

Star wagged his tail in agreement.

Sam headed for his own cabin, sneaking down halls and ducking behind potted palms when anyone passed.

There wasn't a proper bathtub in the suite he shared with his guardian, Lady Lavinia Ulster Cabot. There was a separate room down the halls for baths and showers. But there was a big porcelain bowl with a tank of fresh water above it, filled daily by their bedroom steward.

Sam cracked open the door of B-47, half expecting

to hear Lady Cabot's shrill voice calling through the connecting door: "Samuel? Is that you? Do bring me a buttermint, that's a dear boy."

Sam held his breath, listening. Lady Cabot had come prepared for lavish dinners and elegant evenings sipping champagne. She hadn't come prepared for rowdy boys and dogs.

Sam heard no sound from the room next door. Lady Cabot seemed to be up and about.

"Come on," Sam whispered, and Star bounded out of the hall into the room. The dog circled the room, sniffing the bed, the dresser, the carpet. A crystal decanter of water stood on the polished mahogany dresser. Sam grabbed it and poured water into a goblet for Star. The dog slurped thirstily, spilling water over the sides.

"Mr. Ismay is definitely going to have to work on your manners." Sam grinned at Star. "We have to hurry. What if he decides to come to the kennel to see you, today of all days? We'd put Finn in a real pickle."

Sam stripped off his cotton shirt, kicked off his shoes, wiggled out of his knickers, and knelt beside Star.

Star circled around and around Sam before finally putting a paw on Sam's knee and tilting his head as if to say, "I'm listening." Sam grabbed Star and wrestled playfully with the dog, rolling back and forth across the thick green-and-black-print carpet, leaving streaks of coal dust everywhere.

"Enough, enough!" Sam laughed as Star pinned him to the floor and licked his face. Now even the dog's tongue was black.

Sam turned the gold spigot to bring water down to the porcelain bowl.

"Get up here." Sam lifted Star's front legs onto the edge of the sink, then grabbed his hindquarters and hoisted them up, pushing Star's front legs all the way into the bowl. Half the water splashed out, and Star tried to catch the flying drops in his mouth, sloshing even more water out of the bowl.

"Would you be still?" Sam felt frustrated. This was impossible.

"All right." Sam lowered the dog to the floor and grabbed a plaid wool blanket off his berth, spreading it across the rug. He scrubbed at the dog's coat with a washcloth, working up lather with a bar of lilac-scented soap he found beside the basin.

He dumped the dark water from the sink into the drainage tank below and filled the bowl again. And again. Every time he wrung out the washcloth, the water in the basin turned black. At this rate, he'd run out of water before he ran out of dirt. He rang the bell for the bedroom steward and soon there was a knock at the door.

Star barked, and Sam squelched over to the door, his underdrawers dripping.

"Yes?" Sam opened the door a crack.

A bedroom steward in a spotless navy blue uniform with two rows of shining gold buttons waited in the hall.

Sam stuck his head out and looked both ways, up and down the hall.

"You rang for a steward, sir?"

Sam nodded and motioned the steward inside. "I think we're running low on water," he whispered.

The steward silently surveyed the wrecked room, the blackened towels, the soot-stained rug, the sodden blanket on the floor, and the wet dog, who all at once gave his fur a wild shake. Dirty water splattered in every direction. The steward wiped a black droplet off his cheek. Then he smiled at Sam.

"I think I can help with this, Master Harris. Let me get some more towels and a mop, and we'll have this place set right again in no time." The steward hurried off to get his supplies. Sam sat down on the damp carpet and draped his arm around Star's shoulders.

"Have you noticed how everyone who works on this ship is always smiling?"

Star whapped his tail twice. Two whaps for yes.

One whap for no. Only a wonder dog like Star could do Morse code with his tail.

The steward slipped back through the open door, one arm loaded with clean towels and the other carrying a brush, a mop, and a bucket that slopped over with soapy water.

"Let's try this, Master Harris."

In only a few minutes, using the mop bucket, with Sam holding Star steady and the steward scrubbing up one side and down the other, the setter looked almost normal. At the steward's urging, Sam ran a wet towel over his own face and poured a pitcher of water over his head, then shook his hair, just like Star.

Sam frowned in the mirror as he scrubbed at the worst of the black streaks, wishing for the hundredth time that his face were more square-jawed and manly, like Bucky's, instead of being small and what his grandmum called "refined." Sam's small nose and big blue eyes had forced him to take the part of Juliet in St. Ives Academy's all-boy production of *Romeo and Juliet*.

Sam stuck his tongue out at his reflection and turned from the mirror.

The steward promised to have the room shipshape again by the time Sam returned from the kennel.

Sam crammed himself into a shirt and a fresh pair

of knickers, combing his unruly hair with his fingers. He slipped on his jacket and checked for his journal in the side pocket.

He ran down the hall with Star leading the way. Lady Cabot was probably already wondering why Sam wasn't at dinner. Maybe she was roaming the decks looking for him. He certainly hoped not. He shivered as he came out on the ship's top deck.

There, staring over the rail, was Lady Cabot, her black velvet coat with its bushy fox collar buttoned all the way up against the chill.

She turned at that moment and spotted them. Star's tail whap-whap-whapped against Sam's leg, probably signaling S.O.S. That was three short, three long, and another three short, just the way Harold Bride, the wireless officer, had shown Sam and Bucky it was done. It was the new code for: "We're in trouble, come quick!" Sam and Star were definitely in trouble.

"Samuel Adams Harris." Lady Cabot frowned. "Where have you been? And what have you gotten into? You look a fright. Have you even spoken to Mr. Ismay about the liberties you're taking with his dog? Have you asked his permission?"

Sam's stomach knotted up. Even Bucky had warned him about spending too much time with Star.

"No," Sam said softly. "I haven't seen Mr. Ismay. I *know* Star's not my dog. I'm just sort of . . . *borrowing* him."

"Well then *return* him to the kennel and come with me. We're almost halfway through this voyage, and you're missing out on so many important social things, Samuel. There's a library on board, you know. You should be reading and studying about America. You will soon need to know about it. But instead, you rush through meals with the"—Lady Cabot sputtered— "rudest manners I've ever seen. Your dear grandmum asked that I train you in the art of gracious dining, but you insist on bolting your food as if . . . as if you *were* a dog, instead of just being overly devoted to one."

Sam looked down at Star. "But the meals take half the day," he protested. Lady Cabot would never understand that he wanted to be with Star more than he wanted anything else the *Titanic* had to offer.

She opened her mouth for more scolding, but Colonel Archibald Gracie had emerged from the gymnasium on the forward part of the boat deck and trotted right over to her. Sweat glistened on the man's forehead, but Lady Cabot fluttered her eyelashes at the old coot.

"Oh, Colonel Gracie, you took me by surprise!" Lady Cabot frowned at Sam and Star, but she practically cooed the words as she turned to the colonel and said sadly, "I was just about to escort my ward to dinner. But I fear he is not presentable in his current condition."

"By jove, he's not the only one!" boomed the colonel, reaching up to wipe sweat off his brow. "I was hoping to join you as soon as I get washed up. Quite a workout on that camel contraption in the gymnasium. Feel as if I've ridden across the Sahara and back in thirty minutes! Come, have a look."

Lady Cabot giggled. Sam could hardly believe it. "It would be lovely to dine together," Lady Cabot said, "but I fear my responsibilities are to this boy and his grandmother, so I must—"

"You must meet your ward at the Grand Staircase," finished Colonel Gracie, with a wink at Sam. "We men will work on getting cleaned up, and you, of course, have only to keep looking as lovely as you already do."

Sam didn't know whether to laugh or lean over the side and throw up. How could such old people—they both had to be at least forty—act so silly?

"Get on with you, lad. Take your dog to the kennel, and meet us at the clock on the landing, sans canine, if you please." He chuckled, as if he were much funnier than Sam thought he was.

The colonel escorted Lady Cabot away down the deck. She clutched his arm and giggled again as he bent to whisper in her ear. She seemed to have forgotten all about Sam.

Sam squatted down and rubbed Star's belly. "You're my good luck charm!" he whispered in the dog's ear. Star whapped Sam's leg with his brilliant Morse code tail.

CHAPTER 5

Dog-Paddling the Atlantic

Saturday, April 13, 1912

Water closed over Sam's head.

He came up, happily sputtering. The water in the indoor swimming bath was warm and relaxing. Sam liked to imagine that if he swam back and forth enough times as the *Titanic* steamed ahead, he would actually be swimming across the Atlantic.

Bucky dog-paddled beside Sam, spouting water into the air just like the humpback whales they'd seen breaching that morning.

"Ta-ra-ra-boom-de-ay, We take a swim today, We were dry yesterday, Don't want to be that way," Bucky sang, making up his own words, as usual, splashing Sam in the face with his feet. Several other passengers ducked as a great splashing war ensued. It might have gone on longer if a steward hadn't warned them to keep the water *in* the bath, or they would have to get *out*.

"This is the life," Bucky enthused as he floated along on his back. "I'd rather be here than in those stinky boiler rooms."

"You sure conned your way out of that one," Sam said.

"That was knowledge, not conning." Bucky grinned. "They wanted my opinion on getting more speed with less shoveling."

"*That*'s a sea tale if I ever heard one!" Sam said, rolling over in the water.

"Star's the only one with a tail around here," Bucky shot back. Then he laughed. "Next time, we should just let Star do all the talking. Since you're so sure that dog can do anything."

"Well, I know he could swim better than you." Sam ducked as Bucky sent a splash his way. He tucked his legs, shooting straight out of the water and diving to the bottom of the bath. Sam kept his eyes closed and slithered along by touch, his hands on the tiles. The saltwater stung if he opened his eyes, not like the pond water at Gramp's. Bucky didn't join him underwater. Although his brawny build made Bucky a natural athlete in sports like soccer, Sam was the better swimmer.

If only I could bring Star down here, Sam thought,

it would be perfect. Setters liked the water. They are retrieving dogs, and Sam felt sure Star could swim like a fish and dive like a porpoise.

Sam shot back to the surface, his arms raised to make a glorious fountain of water. He and Bucky settled down into a backstroke race but soon abandoned it when they bumped into some other men in the bath.

The boys climbed out and grabbed the thick Turkish towels provided by the steward. Then they dangled their feet over the high edge and watched a man do the breaststroke, his black bathing cap bobbing up and down like a black rubber ball. Their own gray wool suits, heavy with water, hung to their ankles instead of their knees now. Only their bathing suit belts kept them from slipping off entirely.

"I have to go help Finn walk the dogs," Sam said. "Want to come?"

"I'd like to." Bucky grinned at Sam and then slid off the edge with a great splash. "But my dad's coming down to 'take the waters.' I'm supposed to wait for him. He said if his son went swimming on a ship in the middle of the ocean, then he should do it, too."

"Your dad's a good man." Sam snapped off his rubber bathing cap.

"I know." Bucky grinned as he floated lazily on his back. "But he gets the rules for American football mixed up with the rules for soccer, and the rules for American baseball mixed up with the rules for cricket. I'm not sure I can turn him into a good American dad."

Sam nodded. He trailed a toe through the water. "At least you have a dad."

"You'll have a new dad, soon. Maybe he won't be so bad. I bet he knows a lot about football and baseball."

"How would I know?" Sam's voice was clipped. "My mother's barely told me anything about him."

"Like mother, like son," Bucky said. "You've never told me much about America. You lived there, but you never tell me anything. And I thought we were supposed to be best friends."

Sam looked down at Bucky. "We *are* best friends. No matter what. I'd tell you about America, but I don't remember a lot. It was big. It snowed in the winter. And I wish I didn't have to go back."

"Yeah, I know. And soon enough I'll see America for myself." Bucky swam to the side of the pool. "So, what do you say? Friends till Niagara Falls?"

"Till Ida hoes," Sam answered.

"Till Mary lands."

"Till Tenny sees."

Sam knelt and they touched elbows.

"Tell Finn I *wanted* to help him, but I came down

with mal de mer." Bucky used Lady Cabot's highfalutin name for seasickness.

Sam got up and flicked his towel at his friend. Bucky dodged sideways in the water. Then he whaled a spurt of water in Sam's direction, and Sam ducked to safety in the changing room, still laughing.

He ran his fingers through his thick hair and slipped into his wool knickers and brown cotton shirt. His hair was rumpled and messy again, but he patted it down as flat as he could get it before hurrying toward the rear elevator.

As he stepped into the elevator, Sam was surprised to see a lady with the Saint Bernard sitting on the bench at the back.

"That's some dog you've got," Sam said. He held out his hand for the dog to sniff, then scratched the big Saint Bernard between his floppy ears.

The lady nodded. "He seems to like you. And he doesn't like just anybody. Toujours is a bit of a one-woman dog. I should introduce myself since you're obviously a fellow dog lover. I'm Ann Isham."

She extended her white-gloved hand. Sam shook it. Sam grinned at her. "I'm Sam Harris, ma'am."

"Well, Sam, I'm taking Toujours up to the kennel for his walk today."

Sam knelt in front of the Saint Bernard and ran his hands over the dog's massive chest and down the thick fur of his back. "I help walk the dogs, but this is the first time I've seen yours."

"I walked him myself at first." Miss Isham laughed. "But the sea air has made him as boisterous as a pup, so I've decided I need some young, strong help."

She offered Sam the dog's leather leash as the elevator wheezed to a stop on the boat deck and the liftboy opened the sliding wooden doors. Toujours pranced around excitedly at the tang of cold, salty air.

"You keep this big dog in your cabin, Miss Isham?" Sam asked. "Where does he sleep?"

"I booked a two-berth cabin, and he takes one bed while I take the other." Miss Isham smiled at Sam so broadly, her cheeks dimpled. "He's a better roommate than most. He doesn't snore."

She leaned close to Sam's ear. "I don't know if you'll understand this, but Toujours is my best friend in all the world."

Sam nodded. "I understand," he said. And he did. He understood perfectly.

CHAPTER 6

All Paws on Deck

Saturday, April 13, 1912

Finn carried a shovel and pail. Sam held the ends of four leather leads balled in his fists. It was sort of like a parade, with the dogs going first, dragging Sam behind. Finn brought up the rear, leading four more dogs.

Sam's four dogs all wanted to go in different directions. Toujours pulled him two steps backward. Sam pulled Toujours two steps forward.

"You've got to make them mind," Finn called from behind.

"Come on." Sam pulled harder on the leashes. Star had already yanked his leash free of Sam's grip, but raced back and forth to lick Sam's hands and check on his progress. He barked encouragement all the way. Dogs and boys finally crowded into the aft elevator. The same liftboy was at the control panel, and he grinned at Finn.

"This elevator smells a mite doggy when your crew gets on," he remarked to Finn, wrinkling his nose. He held up a small bottle of lavender cologne. "The purser said to sprinkle this around as soon as you get off. Can't have these fine second-class ladies and gents thinking they're sharing space with dogs, now, can we?"

All the dogs belonged to *first*-class passengers and Sam was certain the liftboy never would have talked this way if Miss Isham had been aboard. Finn countered, "Maybe you could put some of that lavender behind your own ears, sweetheart. Your passengers will be so busy wondering why you smell so sweet, they won't have time to notice the doggy odor."

The liftboy made a halfhearted lunge at Finn's neck as the elevator arrived on C-deck. It opened into a narrow corridor next to the well deck and the second class passenger quarters.

"He'll get over it," Finn said, laughing.

Sam always felt a flurry of excitement in his belly when they crossed the well deck and climbed the steep stairs to the poop deck, the raised deck at the stern of the ship. This time, Toujours needed a boost from behind. The chow and Pye handled the stairs well, as did Star. But Sam had to carry the little King Charles spaniels, one under each arm, as he struggled up the stairs in a tangle of dogs and leashes.

Several children were watching them, from both A- and B-decks. One boy yelled, "That's my dog you've got! Take good care of him!"

Finn squinted up at their audience. "Pay him no mind, Sam. That's Willie Carter. His family owns those little spaniels, and mostly keeps 'em in their rooms. But he doesn't like cleaning up after 'em, so he brings the pair to the kennel for us to walk."

"Hello, little dogs! Hello!" This time it was a girl waving at them.

"Which dog is yours?" Sam called.

"Oh, I don't have a dog," the girl blushed. "But I like the little flat-faced dog with the big ears."

"This one?" Sam picked up Pye, Mr. Daniel's bulldog.

"Oh yes!" The girl clapped her hands together. "How beautiful you are! I love you!"

"Well, that's the closest *you'll* ever get to hearing a girl say 'I love you,'" Finn teased. "Even if she is only five."

"She's at least seven," Sam said stoutly. "Maybe even eight."

"Oooooo!" Finn joked. "Just the right age for a man like you!"

"Cut it out," Sam ordered as Finn flushed the deck clean with his pail.

"All right. Better to have dogs for company at your age anyway," Finn said. "Do you only like dogs? Or cats, too?"

"I never had a cat," Sam said. "I've heard there's one on every ship, though. My gramp told me that ships carry cats for good luck and to catch the rats and mice, but my grandmum said there wouldn't be any rats on the *Titanic*."

"There's rats on every ship that ever sailed," Finn said. They'd led the dogs around the deck three times, and now they made their way back to the stairs. "A rat ran across the third-class dining saloon last night and near caused the ladies a screaming fit. Wish I'd have seen that."

Sam took the spaniels down the stairs to the well deck and tied them to the rail. He came back up to get Toujours. The dog seemed to be all legs and tail, and he felt as heavy as a grown man. Wherever Sam went, up or down, Star followed.

"Why didn't the *Titanic*'s cat catch the rat?" Sam asked.

"Because nobody's seen a whisker of that cat since we got under way." Finn shook his head. "Can't figure it out. Neither can the other ship's boys. But there better be a cat aboard. It's downright unlucky to have a maiden voyage without a ship's cat. We're bound to find the creature by the time we get to America and everybody gets off, if not before."

Sam didn't ever want to get off the *Titanic*. That would mean seeing his mother again, and meeting his new stepfather, Jack. Sam's stomach twisted painfully.

There were only a few things Sam was sure he could count on in life. Bucky was one. He could also count on his grandparents, or at least he'd thought he could until they agreed to send him back to America. He could count on the *Titanic*, since it was the finest ship ever made.

Most of all, he could count on Star.

Finn was nowhere in sight after dinner that night, but Sam left his friend two marzipan fruits from the dessert tray, wrapped in a cloth napkin on the dogs' feeding counter. The kennel was unusually quiet, with Toujours, Frou-Frou, the Pomeranians Lady Jane and Aggie, and both of the Carter family spaniels off in their owners' cabins. Only J. J. Astor's two Airedales; Chester, the fox terrier; Rufus, the chow; Pye; and Star were in their cages.

Sam opened Star's cage and the dog shot out in a flurry of fur. Star licked Sam's hands and stood on his hind legs, trying to lick his face. Finally, he calmed down enough for Sam to reach into his pocket. "Here you go."

He pulled out a steak bone with sirloin still clinging to it. With an eager snuffle, Star fell to chewing, stretching out on the green-and-white linoleum floor. "So that's the trick," Sam said. "Give you a bone and all of a sudden you get all quiet and polite." Sam stretched out beside Star, his head pillowed on the dog's side, and let his mind float with the ship.

The warm closeness of the kennel air was comforting after the cold winds on the boat deck. Sam draped his arm over Star's back and curled closer.

The setter turned away from the bone, just for a moment, and nuzzled Sam gently. Then he went back to chewing, the sound of his gnawing teeth blending with the sound of the thrumming engines far below. Sam's eyes closed as he fit his head more snugly into the hollow of Star's body.

Within seconds, he was asleep.

CHAPTER 7

Canine Detectives
Sunday, April 14, 1912

Sam was only a little bit stiff from sleeping on the kennel floor. Mostly it was his ear that was sore, because Lady Cabot had nearly twisted it off when she found him.

"Young gentlemen do not lie down with beasts," she yelled as she hauled him off for a bath. Then she made him attend the church services in the Grand Salon.

Captain Smith was presiding, and he was probably the best preacher Sam had ever heard. No sermon at all. Just a few hymns, a few words about a safe voyage, a prayer, then a final hymn about "those in peril on the sea."

Sam didn't glance back at Lady Cabot after the last *amen*. He charged out the doors and up the Grand

Staircase. Bucky was waiting for him in the kennel, sitting on the floor with Star. He looked up at Sam and nodded.

"Yeah, my folks made me go, too. But I snuck out during the third hymn. I knew you'd come here."

Star bounded over to Sam, nudging his hands and circling him joyfully.

"I'm lucky to be alive. I didn't think Lady Cabot would ever let up."

Bucky grinned. "You should have seen her at our cabin door this morning. She was nearly hyperventilating. 'Sam's gone overboard! I can't find him anywhere. He hasn't even slept in his bed.' She kept yelling until I told her to check the kennel. Otherwise, she would've fainted for sure."

"Maybe you shouldn't have told her," Sam said. "It could have saved her twisting off my ear if I'd had more time to think of a good excuse for being out all night."

"Then *my* mother would have twisted *my* ear," Bucky replied, practical as always.

"So what's the plan?" Sam asked. Star's rear leg thumped on the linoleum as Sam dug his fingers into Star's thick fur and scratched the sweet spot on his back.

"Today we check the lifeboats. I figure that ship's cat might be holed up in one of them. Nobody would ever think to look for her there." Bucky pulled a battery torch from his pocket. "We'll even search the hold, crate by crate, if we have to."

Sam heard the ringing of nine bells—nine o'clock. It was hard to tell what the proper time was on the ship, since time kept changing as they moved across the Atlantic. Bucky said the *Titanic* had 48 clocks. A trumpeter played "Oh! The Roast Beef of England" before every meal, marching up and down the A-deck promenade as he blew the call to breakfast, lunch, or dinner. The call for breakfast was sounding now, but Bucky pulled two rolls and two chocolate bars out of his pocket.

"I thought ahead," he said wisely. "Let's go."

They had to hunt to find a deserted spot on the boat deck. Sunday strollers were everywhere, despite the nip in the air. Sam and Star ducked behind a lifeboat and kept watch while Bucky unhooked a corner of the canvas tarpaulin that covered the boat.

They boosted Star inside and slipped in after him. It was so dark under the canvas cover that Bucky clicked on his torch.

There were benches and storage boxes—not much else. Star had his nose glued to a spot right in the middle of the lifeboat's floor.

"Has he found the cat?" Bucky asked hopefully.

Sam crawled forward and pushed Star aside.

45

"It's a hole!" he exclaimed, forgetting to whisper. "In the bottom of the lifeboat!"

Bucky crawled forward to look. Star's wet nose rested against Sam's cheek as they all studied the hole.

"There's only one possible explanation," Bucky announced grimly. "The crew is planning to send all the passengers off in lifeboats, pretending we're sinking. Then, when everyone else is off the ship, they'll steal all the jewels and furs and rich people's stuff."

"Like we'd be stupid enough to believe the *Titanic* could sink?" Sam snorted contemptuously.

Bucky stuck a finger through the hole and wiggled it around. Star flopped down, stretched out, and yawned.

"This is no time for a nap, Star," Bucky scolded. "We've uncovered a scandal."

"Got you!"

The voice from outside the boat made Sam jump.

"Hey!" Bucky tried to pull back his finger, but someone outside had ahold of it. There was a rapping on the lifeboat, and Star began to bark a greeting.

Then Bucky's finger was free and Robert Daniel was stripping back the canvas cover. Sunlight flooded in on them.

Pye leaped higher than Sam would've thought possible and landed on top of Bucky's head.

"Oosh!" Bucky's face was smushed against the lifeboat's floor.

"Wouldn't a nice game of quoits be a better way to pass a Sunday afternoon, gentlemen?" Mr. Daniel asked. There was laughter in his voice. "Or at least, a way that wouldn't get you in trouble?"

"But look what we found!" Sam pointed at the hole as Bucky rolled off it. Pye covered Bucky's spluttering lips with doggy kisses.

"It's a conspiracy," Bucky announced, pushing Pye aside. "The crew plans to steal the jewels and money of swells like J. J. Astor and Benjamin Guggenheim, while we"—Bucky tapped his chest for emphasis—"the witnesses, sink to the bottom in these holey lifeboats."

Mr. Daniel held up a piece of cork hanging from the side of the lifeboat on a thin chain. "You don't suppose you could plug the hole with this?" he asked and grinned.

"But why . . ." Sam began.

"Drainage. It rains. The sea gets rough and water splashes into the lifeboats. Drainage holes keep them dry and ready. When they're lowered, a crewman plugs up the hole with this cork as easily as you put a stopper in your bathtub." Mr. Daniel scooped up Pye into his arms.

"Oh," Bucky said. "You know so much. Do you

know where the ship's cat is?" He crossed his arms over his chest, waiting.

Sam and Star jumped from the gunwale of the lifeboat to the boat deck as Bucky sat pouting.

"The ship's cat? No idea. But trust me, lads, it's around here somewhere. No crew in the world would sail without one. Sailors," he added, lowering his voice, "are a superstitious lot."

Mr. Daniel walked them back to the kennel, a hand on both their slumped shoulders. "I'm sorry, boys. It did make a good story, sailing with a pirate crew planning to steal all the ship's riches. You investigated and you got the facts. Isn't it better to know the truth? That way you can meet things head on. Most of the time, the truth turns out not to be as bad as you think it is."

Sam could feel Mr. Daniel's eyes on him. He wondered, not for the first time, how much gossiping Lady Cabot had been doing about Sam's mother and Jack, and what Sam might have to face in America.

"Yeah," Bucky agreed sullenly. "But a *little* conspiracy would have been interesting."

Mr. Daniel slapped Sam on the back. "Too much thinking. That's what we're doing. Right, Sam?"

Sam nodded as they separated, Mr. Daniel heading for the gym, and the boys going down to the galleys to try and beg a biscuit apiece.

It was after dinner before they returned to the kennel. Mr. Daniel was there, too. Sam said good night to Star. The dog clearly believed he should be at Sam's side every minute. Finally, the boys did their double-elbow salute and headed out, leaving Mr. Daniel sitting on Pye's crate with the dog in his lap and an unlit cigar jutting from the corner of his mouth. "Good night, boys," he called. "If Bruce Ismay has his way, we'll steam into New York harbor Tuesday for sure."

Sam didn't want to think about reaching New York. Bucky and he played a game of quoits with two American boys who seemed to think they were playing horseshoes and argued that getting the rope circle *close* to the pegs should count for points. Bucky lectured the Yanks long and hard on the rules of the British game. The Americans finally conceded defeat and left.

When Sam returned to his cabin, he heard the unmistakable high-pitched whistling-wheeze of Lady Cabot's snore. It was late and Sam was tired, but he wanted to write in his notebook before he fell asleep. He had to fight to keep his eyes open, but he was determined not to miss an entry. He lifted his pencil to the paper. "It was cold today, Gramp. Cold enough for a muffler and gloves, even though it must be spring back home at your house."

Sam's pencil jumped, making the "e" in *house* curl up around the page.

He'd felt something strange, he was sure of it. It was a sensation like skating in leather-soled shoes across a floor covered with marbles. He heard something, too. A creak? A groan? A scraping noise?

They were in the middle of the Atlantic Ocean. There was nothing out there to scrape against.

Sam threw back his blanket and climbed over the side of his berth. He opened his porthole, gasping as the frigid night air struck him in the face. Glancing left and then right, Sam blinked. Was that a sail? It was large and white. He looked again, but it was gone.

Sam was wide awake now. He grabbed his shoes and pulled them on, stuffing the laces in the sides.

Flinging open his cabin door, he heard the Bishops' little white dog, Frou-Frou, barking wildly from across the hall.

A steward came hurrying down the hall with stacks of towels in both hands. He was frowning.

"What *was* that?" Sam asked. "What happened?" His voice sounded unnaturally loud in the long corridor.

The steady thrum of the engines had stopped completely, and the silence was so sudden, it roared in Sam's ears.

"Nothing to worry about, Master Harris. We may have dropped a propeller, is all. We'll be under way again before you can pop into some clothes and go check on that dog you're so fond of."

Sam smiled. "How did you know that's what I was thinking?"

"I was young myself once. I haven't forgotten entirely. Dress warmly now. It's colder than an ice house in January up above, and that's a fact. The order has come down to put on life vests, just as a routine precaution. Yours is on top of your wardrobe."

"Life vests? We're not sinking, are we?"

The steward began to laugh. "Sure, and I'd be taking the time to deliver towels to the Astors on C-deck if we were sinking, now, wouldn't I?" He winked at Sam, giving him a cheerful smile. "It's the rules and regulations that tell us what to do, and life vests are the rule for anything that would make us come to a full stop. So put yours on and be done with it!"

Sam nodded and ducked back into his cabin. Sailors had more rules than the headmaster at St. Ives. He slipped the bulky canvas life vest on over his head. It felt awkward and stiff as he tied the lace in the front around the top of his red long johns.

The silence had been quickly replaced by the whoosh of steam blasting out of the ship's funnels. It sounded like a hundred trains blaring their whistles in chorus. The noise was bound to drive Star and the other dogs crazy.

Sam listened at the door to Lady Cabot's cabin. She was still snoring. He wouldn't wake her up just for a dropped propeller.

He'd only be gone long enough to make sure Star was all right. He would have forgotten his coat if it hadn't been for the steward's earlier reminder. His wool dress coat didn't fit well over the life vest, so Sam didn't button it.

As he went down the hall, Sam could still hear Frou-Frou. The Bishops would never be able to sleep through that. Frou-Frou had always been a barker. But tonight the little dog was barking as if her life depended on it.

CHAPTER 8

"Not Without My Dog"

Monday, April 15, 1912, 12:30 A.M.

Sam wasn't worried.

The officers seemed busy, but they didn't look worried, either. As for the passengers, some looked irritated by the delay, and others looked amused at this bit of adventure on the high seas.

On the boat deck, there were women in bare feet with black beaver coats over their silky ankle-length nightgowns. There were children in footed pajamas, wrapped in navy blue blankets taken right off their beds. Most people were wearing the canvas and cork life vests.

Steam blowing through the towering funnels in an endless, earsplitting blast made conversation impossible.

Sam was glad he was wearing his red long johns under his coat because it was bitterly cold, just as the steward had said. Sam's feet without stockings were freezing inside his leather shoes.

Mr. Daniel was wearing his white woolen long johns and a pair of polished black shoes without any socks. A thick deck rug was wrapped around his shoulders. Sam wasn't surprised to see that Mr. Daniel had taken the time to grab his derby. The dapper banker was never without his hat.

The noisy steam blast finally stopped and voices started up at once. Mr. Daniel smiled at Sam. "It's a come-as-you-are party, lad!" He laughed. "I think I'm wearing the winning getup! What do you say, Sam?"

"I don't know, sir. The sailors are taking the covers off the lifeboats. I heard one of them saying, 'Women and children first.' Do you think something's *really* wrong?"

"Oh, you know the Brits, son. Nothing will do but to follow the rules, no matter how cold and dark the night. I'm sure it's just a precautionary thing. Well, listen to that, Sam. The band's playing 'Oh You Beautiful Doll.' The band wouldn't be playing if this were a real emergency, now would it?"

"I suppose not, sir."

Despite Mr. Daniel's suggestion that things were fine, he steered Sam toward Lifeboat Number 7, which was already being loaded. Most people were hanging back, however, unwilling to leave the safety of the brightly lit boat deck for the black water far below. Women clung to their husbands, refusing to get in. Children clung to their mothers. Sam glimpsed Miss Isham clinging to Toujours. The crowd parted and closed ranks again as Mr. Ismay himself appeared, urging everyone to make haste and board the lifeboats. Sam recognized the president of the White Star Line from seeing him in the dining saloon. But now no one paid the man any attention. Sam took a step toward Mr. Ismay. This was his chance to talk to him about Star, but before he could, Mr. Daniel stepped in, pushing Sam along. "Get on with you now, lad. Wouldn't do to buck the captain's orders. Women and children first."

Sam twisted out of Mr. Daniel's grasp with a quick dodge.

"No time for games now, Sam. Get back over here."

"Are *you* getting in?" Sam challenged.

"Do I look like a woman?" Mr. Daniel reached for Sam and the deck rug fell off his shoulders. A woman standing just behind them grabbed it off the deck and wrapped it around a small child who was already so heavily bundled, his sleepy little face could barely be seen.

"Do *I* look like a child?" Sam yelled, backing away.

Mr. Daniel stared at Sam, the exasperation on his

face giving way to his familiar wide grin. "All right. You're not a child."

"That's right. I'm . . ." Sam hesitated. "Fourteen."

"If you're fourteen," Mr. Daniel returned, "I'm a codfish's uncle. You told me when we first met that you were twelve."

"*I'm* fourteen," Bucky said, coming up beside them. "Sam is twelve. But he's as smart as fourteen."

Sam grimaced. Bucky wasn't helping.

"They'll take a twelve-year-old," Mr. Daniel said quietly. "There's a place in the lifeboats for you. You'd be foolish not to take it, Sam."

"But the men are staying here," Sam insisted.

Mr. Daniel finally shrugged, although a cloud of worry passed over his face. "Well then, don't just stand there like a binnacle bolted to the deck. Let's help the women and children get this drill over and done."

It was almost like a big game, thought Sam, with people joking and teasing. "Oh, you'll be back on board for breakfast, Lily," a lady in a red satin evening dress called to another in a blanket and flannel nightgown. "And you'll find me right here, all warm and toasty, dancing with the gents to that grand orchestra." She gestured gaily to the ship's band, which was playing the "Merry Widow Waltz." "Don't forget your ticket, Lil. You'll need it to get back on board!"

The music changed and Bucky sang with complete cheerfulness. "Ta-ra-ra-boom-de-ay, If we go down today, I'll swim the other way, Ta-ra-ra-boom-de-ay."

Sam approached Ismay again and almost ended up being thrown into a lifeboat for his trouble. Ismay grabbed Sam's shoulders and began to propel him toward another boat. The man's long mustache drooped over his mouth, unwaxed and trembling. "Get in, get in, you must all get in," Ismay mumbled, lifting Sam right off his feet to swing him toward the lifeboat.

Sam kicked out desperately, hitting a foot against the back of a soot-stained stoker who had just come up on deck. He had to get to Star. Ismay lost his grip and Sam tumbled backward, almost landing in an offi-cer's lap.

"No time for tomfoolery," scolded the officer. "Get out of the way there, boy, and let the women through."

"Hurry, hurry, get them into the boats," panted Ismay as he pushed one woman and pulled another toward the lifeboat. "Are there any more women?" he called.

A woman's long skirts swept past Sam where he sat on the deck beside an abandoned pile of French bread, the loaves dumped haphazardly where some scullery boy had left them while trying to load the lifeboats with supplies. Sam reached out and jammed a flattened loaf into his coat pocket for Star.

"Here," called one woman, but as Ismay grabbed her hand she added, "but I'm only a stewardess."

"Never mind," Ismay told her. "You must take your place."

First Officer Murdoch stood nearby, supervising the loading of all the starboard boats.

"Lower away," Ismay commanded him.

Officer Murdoch looked at Ismay with a carefully expressionless face. A sailor, after all, didn't take orders from a passenger, even if that passenger owned the boat.

"I await my captain's orders," the officer announced.

But Ismay was not to be put off. Clinging to a davit bent under the weight of the loaded lifeboat, he screamed, "Lower away! Lower away!"

A crewman working with the boat's ropes exploded: "If you'll get out of the way, I'll be able to get something done! If I lower away too quickly, I'll drown the whole lot of them!"

Ismay stood rooted to the deck as if someone had slapped him across the face. His eyes darted from the officers to the other passengers, and he let out a groan. Without another word, he turned away from the lifeboats and disappeared into the crowd.

Sam scrambled to his feet. He needed to find Star, because this didn't feel like a drill anymore.

"Officer Pitman! You're in charge of this lifeboat," barked Officer Murdoch to the crewman. "You know who that was, don't you?" he said, nodding in the direction Ismay had gone.

Pitman shrugged and moved to the tiller as the lowering started.

Murdoch continued, "That was our boss, Pitman. You just bawled out Mr. J. Bruce Ismay himself."

"Wouldn't matter if he was the Pope himself," Pitman replied. "My only boss is Captain Smith and the other ship's officers, and we're only going to get one chance to do this right."

"Look sharp now," Murdoch told him. He walked beside the lowering lifeboat and raised a hand to Pitman in a sort of half salute. "Good-bye, Pitman. And good luck."

A whistle blew behind Sam as Pitman and another crewman scrambled around in their boat to find the plug.

"Where's the confounded plug?" Pitman shouted, followed by another blast on the officer's whistle.

"See to the plug!" hollered another voice.

Sam fought his way across the crowded deck to the port side, and suddenly Bucky was at his elbow again. His mother, Mrs. Kingsbury, was trying to wrap her arms around both Sam and Bucky and pull them toward the next lifeboat.

"Dad is putting us in a boat," Bucky explained, looking a bit sheepish. "Ma says you're to come with us."

"Not without Star," Sam said flatly.

Bucky nodded. He understood.

They were almost at the head of the line now, and Mrs. Kingsbury stepped over the gunwale of the lifeboat and reached for Bucky and Sam. But an officer laid a hand on Bucky's shoulder, stopping him.

"You can go." He nodded at Sam. "But not you," he said to Bucky. "Women and children first."

"*No-o-o!*" Mrs. Kingsbury screamed. "My son! Let me have my son, officer. He's only twelve. He's big for his age."

"*He's* twelve," Bucky corrected her, pointing at Sam with frustrated anger in his voice. "*I'm* fourteen."

The starchy officer gave Sam a shove forward, but Sam spun aside.

"He means *I'm* fourteen and *he's* twelve," Sam said, thinking quickly. "Our mother is right. He's big for his age."

Mr. Kingsbury pulled Bucky out from under the officer's grip, calling out to his wife: "Buckthorn and Samuel and I will be fine, Gladys. You go along and we'll see you when they get this all sorted out. I won't let anything happen to the boys. Don't worry, my dear. Everything will be fine, you'll see."

Mrs. Kingsbury was sobbing loudly as the lifeboat was lowered. "Oh, Webb, we'll never get to New York on time now. Everything must be repacked; we must wire the hotel," she called. Her voice faltered. "You will be coming in a later boat, Webb? You and the boys will meet me?"

It was a long, scary way down to the water. Mr. Kingsbury only nodded. It didn't seem fair, if there was nothing really wrong, to tear families apart, making children wail and women cry.

"What did you do that for?" Bucky loomed over Sam. "You *know* I'm fourteen."

"I was trying to help your mum get you into that boat with her. Couldn't you see how scared she was? She *needed* you."

Bucky's right hand balled into a fist. "Yeah, well, I'm not getting in one of those boats unless Dad does. Got it?"

Sam laid a hand on his friend's arm. "I should have known you wouldn't go when all the other men are staying. If I feel that way, I should have known you would, too. I'm sorry." Sam offered Bucky his hand. "Still friends?"

Bucky smiled slowly. He and Sam bumped elbows in the old familiar way, first one, then the other.

"Till Niagara Falls."

"Till Lands End," Sam answered.

"Till the Swansea."

"Till the Killy begs."

They heard a commotion not far from where they stood. "Isn't that the lady with the Saint Bernard?" Bucky asked.

Sam pushed his way through the crowd of men and boys, closer to the spot where Ann Isham knelt beside Toujours. An officer was pulling her by the arm, but she stubbornly clung to her dog's neck.

"You *must* get into the boat, madam," a deck steward insisted. "It's about to be lowered. You must come immediately."

"No!" Miss Isham's voice was determined. "If there's no room for Toujours, then I'm not going, either. I am *not* going without my dog."

"Fine. Stay with your dog, lady," the steward said, dropping her arm in disgust. "If that's what you want, that's the way it'll be. But we're not letting dogs into the lifeboats."

Sam's stomach twisted. "Miss Isham, I'm going over to the kennel to check on Star. I could take Toujours with me," Sam offered.

There were tears running down Miss Isham's cheeks. "You're a dear boy," she said. "But Toujours stays with me. See to yourself, Sam. Please. Be safe."

Sam nodded and turned to Bucky. "Want to come with me?"

"He's not going anywhere." Mr. Kingsbury had his hand on Bucky's shoulder. "And neither are you, Sam. Do you hear what they're saying? This ship hit an iceberg. That's a serious matter, if it's true. We have to stick together. We have to be ready."

"It's all right. I'll be back," Sam assured him.

"Stay here, Sam," Mr. Kingsbury said firmly.

But Sam was already threading his way through the crowd.

He was surprised to see some of the people from steerage on the deck now. One of them was carrying a chunk of ice the size of a soccer ball in both hands. "Brought it up from the well deck," Sam heard him say. "Some of the lads down there had a bit of fun with these blighters, kicking them to and fro. We surely shaved off a boatload of ice when we scraped that berg."

"You're coming back, aren't you?" Bucky called after Sam.

"I'll be right back, Buck. I'll bring Star."

CHAPTER 9

🐾

Boys and Dogs First

Monday, April 15, 1912, 1:30 A.M.

"Sam! Samuel Harris! Over here!"

The crowd parted for an instant and Sam caught sight of Lady Cabot. The ruffled neck and smocking of her flannel nightgown were visible under her coat, mostly because she'd only buttoned one button, and she'd gotten that one wrong. On her head perched her blue velvet wide-brimmed hat with two white turtledoves on top. She was standing up in a lifeboat just starting to be lowered over *Titanic*'s side. Several people in the boat were pulling on her, trying to make her sit down. She started shrieking and beating on the chest of a man in uniform, who was trying hard to restrain her.

"Sit down or you'll make the boat tilt!" he yelled into her face.

"*You* said my ward was *already* on a lifeboat, but there he is!" She pointed up at Sam. "You will *stop* this boat this instant!" she commanded. "I cannot leave this ship without my ward. I have given my word to his grandmum!"

The man shoved Lady Cabot down between two other women on one of the lifeboat's benches. "You're crazy if you think we're stopping this boat. Sit down and shut your mouth."

Sam looked over the rail. He could practically feel the heat from the steam he knew must be coming out of Lady Cabot's ears. Without warning, she lunged at the side of the lifeboat, trying to catch hold of the A-deck rail they were passing as the lifeboat was lowered.

The sailor pulled her back, and she began beating on his chest again, screaming, "Samuel Harris is my responsibility! I'm coming, Sam! I'm coming! I *must* go back!"

"Lady, you ain't going nowhere!" the sailor bellowed. He pushed her onto the bench and sat down on top of her, pinning her to the seat. Lady Cabot peered desperately around the man's shoulder. She raised her hat and waved it at Sam.

"Find a lifeboat, quickly, Samuel! I'll be waiting for you!"

"I'll be all right!" Sam called back. "Don't worry."

Then Lady Cabot's lifeboat was bobbing on the water and the sailors were unhooking it from the davit ropes. As it rowed away, Sam could still see Lady Cabot's white face staring up at him.

"This way!" A man's voice came from right behind him. "They're loading another lifeboat. You're young enough. I'm sure they'll take you. I'll say you're my son. We have to hurry. Come on."

The man made a grab for Sam's arm but caught only air. Sam had already darted away.

The kennel was unnaturally quiet after the music and voices on the boat deck. No one was barking, although Sam could hear Kitty, one of J. J. Astor's beloved Airedales, whining in the big cage in the corner. Mr. Daniel was already there. Pye's cage was open, and Mr. Daniel had gathered the little bulldog into his arms and was crooning into one of his big saucer ears.

The fat stogie still stuck out of the corner of Mr. Daniel's mouth. A faint cloud of smoke already hung in the air. It was against all the rules to smoke in the kennel, but Mr. Daniel was smoking anyway.

All the dogs were crowding nervously in the front of their cages. The chow was pacing back and forth. Star stood with his nose pressed between the wooden dowels of his cage door. He whined as he caught sight of Sam.

"Thought I might see you here, Sam," Mr. Daniel said. "Suppose there's a special lifeboat set aside for our canine friends? Or at least"—Mr. Daniel gave a snort of laughter—"the females among them?"

"What's happening, Mr. Daniel?" Sam opened Star's door and Star surged forward, pressing against Sam's legs.

"Hard to say, lad." Mr. Daniel didn't meet Sam's eyes as he answered. He kept looking at Pye. "I wonder if those in charge are telling us all they know. I've got a bad feeling about this one. These dogs know something's afoot. Something big." He finally looked up. "Don't mean to alarm you, son, but you asked."

"Where's Finn?"

"The boy who works in here? I saw him down in the lobby with the other ship's boys and the elevator lads. They were having themselves a bit of a smoke."

Sam's mouth fell open. If Finn MacDougal was smoking a cigarette in *Titanic*'s first-class lobby . . . , it *was* the end of the world.

Sam grabbed a leather lead from the hook by the kennel door and quickly attached it to Star's collar.

When Mr. Daniel only stared at him, Sam said, "I'm not leaving Star behind, no matter what the officers say."

Mr. Daniel shook his head. "They don't even have room for all the passengers, son. Looks like it's the *Titanic* that'll be leaving us behind. Men and dogs both."

"But all those lifeboats . . ." Sam's protest was loud, almost a shout.

"Did you count them? This ship has a swimming bath, a gymnasium, and even a squash court, for those of us who like a little exercise to go with our caviar and champagne." Mr. Daniel's voice had dropped to a hoarse whisper. "But not enough lifeboats. Not nearly enough." He nodded at Sam encouragingly. "Though *you* might still have time to get into one, if you hurry."

Sam looked down at Star and a shudder of fear ran through him. "I can't leave Star," he whispered.

"I'll take care of your dog, son. Don't you worry about White Star. Old Ismay wouldn't let his prize pooch go down with his ship, any more than I'd let the most expensive French bulldog the world has ever known get even one toe of his championship paws wet. Take my word for it, Sam, you run now. Catch a lifeboat."

Sam didn't move. How was Mr. Daniel going to save Pye—and Star—if they weren't letting men or dogs into the lifeboats? It didn't matter if you were a Philadelphia banker or the president of the White Star Line, or even the captain of the *Titanic* itself. None of them could do anything. They weren't admitting the *Titanic* was going down, but it was. All of them would soon be floating in what Bucky, in his usually endless spiel of information, had said was twenty-eight-degree–Fahrenheit water and unless another ship came along soon . . . Sam didn't allow himself to finish the thought.

"I need a vest for Star. I think I saw a couple on deck," Sam said. He turned to the door of the kennel, his fingers wrapped securely around Star's leash. Maybe, if Star was floating on a life vest, he would survive. Sam pulled the door open. "I'll get one for Pye, too," he added, without looking back at Mr. Daniel. It was better not to meet his eyes.

"Take care, son," Mr. Daniel called. "And if you're ever in Philadelphia, be sure to look me—"

But Sam didn't hear the rest. Star lunged forward, almost yanking Sam off his feet. The leather lead played out like the line of a fishing reel as the dog pulled Sam along the boat deck. Sam ran, an awkward, stumbling lope that barely kept up with Star's frantic pace. He wanted to whistle the dog to a stop, but he couldn't catch his breath. Star dragged him down the sloping deck, where ocean water was creeping up on them from the already covered bridge below.

"S-S-Star!" Sam managed to stutter.

The end of the leash slipped from his fingers with a final jerk and Sam sprawled headfirst into a forest of legs.

Star skidded to a stop and hurled his body around, running right over Sam's shoulders and standing for a moment on Sam's rump, surveying the scene.

"Star." Sam struggled to his knees and threw his arms around the dog's neck, looping the leash over his wrist, tightly this time.

Star barked twice and plunged right through the crowd, pulling Sam to his feet. Sam ran, smashing into folks right and left.

It was only the fear twisting in Sam's gut that kept the whole thing from being funny. Sam began to hiccup. The hiccups strangled deep in Sam's throat as Star reached the edge of the deck. With the lifeboats gone, there was nothing there. No railing. No rope. Nothing but open space.

Star sailed off the edge straight into the starry sky.

Sam went right behind him.

He was too surprised to scream or shout or make any noise at all. He splashed into an endless ocean of blackness. Hitting the water was like breaking through a crust of ice into a frozen pond, as Sam had done once, long ago, while skating with his father. He half expected to feel his father's strong hands, as he'd felt them then, fishing him out, wrapping him in his own dry coat, and hurrying him to the bonfire on shore.

But there was no shore here. No bonfire. No one to rescue him.

Sam's head clunked against something hard as he plunged down. The cold water pricked his flesh like a thousand needles. His woolen coat was an anchor now, dragging him farther and farther into the never-ending darkness.

Sam flailed and kicked. He could hear no sound. He could see no lights. He didn't know which way was up.

He shrugged out of one sleeve of his coat before he realized something was wrapped around his right hand.

It was the end of Star's leather lead.

It was his lifeline.

The lead jerked and Sam's right hand, still encased in the tangling coat, lost its grip and came loose. Sam grabbed onto the lead desperately with his freed left hand. His lungs were about to burst. Any moment now, he'd open his mouth to gulp a breath.

His right arm dragged behind him, and the unbuttoned coat floated free. Sam shot up like a cork, breaking the surface with barely a splash.

Reflections of the ship's glittering portholes shone across the eerily calm water. Wet fur rubbed Sam's cheek as he sucked in air. He tried to fill his empty lungs all in one breath and ended up swallowing a mouthful of

71

seawater. His forehead throbbed over his right eye, and when he felt the spot, it was warm and sticky.

He reached for Star, whose head was the only part visible above the swells. Several deck chairs floated around them, shadowy in the ship's light.

Sam's life vest helped hold him up, but Star was right there under Sam's trembling hands, like a life preserver of hope in this vast empty ocean.

Sam stared up at the *Titanic*. The bow dipped so low, the ship looked like a duck sticking its head under the water with its tail feathers high in the air.

The *Titanic* was sinking. It was impossible. But it was happening right before his eyes.

His teeth were chattering, and Sam had to blink away a sudden sleepiness that swept over him. He'd been so cold. But he was starting to feel warmer now.

Star was dog-paddling with powerful strokes, pulling Sam along. Sam had no idea where Star was going, but he kicked his feet feebly, trying to help.

"Over here! This way!" The voice sounded far away. Sam couldn't even tell from what direction the faint cry came. His head seemed to be full of cotton. Water sloshed against his ears and he tried to shake it out, but he ended up dunking his head back under.

"That's the way, lad. Swim this way. Come on. Come on, we've almost got you."

Sam's legs trailed in the water behind the motor of Star's paddling paws. The shoes he'd pulled on in his cabin were gone. At least he thought they were gone. Sam couldn't really feel his feet.

His head clunked into something. Wasn't that just the way? A person could be floating in the middle of the North Atlantic, watching his ship go down, and some hard thing knocked him in the head. Was this any way to run an ocean?

"I've got him." The man's voice was right above him. An angel, maybe, swooping down from heaven. Or maybe a big fish, letting his buddies down below know he'd caught a delicious frozen boy. "Come on now, son, give us some help."

There was the pressure of hands on Sam's arms, and the neck of his long johns pulled tight. Someone slapped him across the face.

"Stay with us. I recognize him. It's Sam Harris, the boy who helped walk the dogs." That voice was Madeleine Astor's, J. J. Astor's pretty young bride with the Airedales. "Come on, Sam, snap out of it," she urged.

"Put your arms up," a man said. "And let go of that dog, before the weight of the two of you makes the whole boat tip."

Sam's arm tightened around Star. His other arm reached up and grabbed the side of the lifeboat.

"Go ahead," Sam choked, finally finding his voice. "Pull us up."

"I'm not taking a dog aboard this boat," answered the man. "There's no room. No room for a dog."

Sam saw only shadowy shapes above him. He was half in the water and half out. His hair dripped frosty rivulets down his face and warm tears ran down his cheeks.

"I'm not leaving my dog. He saved my life, and I'm not leaving him." Sam didn't ask. He didn't beg. He just stated the facts.

"There's no room for a dog," the man repeated. There seemed to be other murmurs, but Sam couldn't make out what was being said.

Then Madeleine Astor spoke in a voice of authority. "The boy won't come without his dog, Quartermaster Perkis, and we're not leaving him here. I left my husband. I left our dogs. I'll pull these two in by myself if you won't help. But I will not allow you to leave them here."

"I'm not saying we're leaving the boy, Mrs. Astor. Just give me a minute to pry him off the dog. Don't worry. I'll get him into the boat."

CHAPTER 10

❖

The Outcry and the Silence

Monday, April 15, 1912, around 2:00 A.M.

Sam tightened his grip on Star. No one could pry Sam away from the dog.

"Pull them both in this minute, Mr. Perkis," Mrs. Astor demanded. "We have more than enough room."

Perkis grumbled and lifted Sam out of the water. With Sam's arms locked around Star, the dog came up right beside him. But Star yelped in pain and frantically began to scramble backward.

"What's the matter, boy?" Sam asked, desperately twisting his hands into the dog's wet fur to hold him "Are you hurt?"

Star dipped back around, nipping at the quartermaster's knee balanced on the gunwale. And then Sam saw the problem.

"His tail is caught!" Sam shouted at Perkis. "In that metal thing. Right under your knee."

"What? I . . . ," Perkis began, but Mrs. Astor was already dislodging the dog's tail from the metal oarlock where it had been pinned.

Star yelped again.

"There, there, you beautiful creature," Mrs. Astor cooed softly. "It's just a bit of fur you've lost." She guided Sam forward and kept him from falling, face-down, onto the floor of the boat. Instead he was lowered slowly and found himself sitting on something soft.

Star was right beside him, whining. The dog twisted around to lick his tail. "I'm afraid his tail might be bent the wrong way," Mrs. Astor whispered, "but it's a small price to pay for having him here."

"Thank you, ma'am."

Sam took Star between his knees to steady him.

The Irish setter ran a warm tongue across Sam's chin and nudged him with his nose. Sam gently felt Star's tail. It was bent at a backward angle, perhaps broken. He hugged the dog close, shivering, his teeth chattering.

"That boy is wearing his underwear, Mama."

"Shush, Ned," came a woman's soft voice. "Don't knock against me so, or you'll wake Georgie." In the darkness, Sam could just make out the shapes of a lady

them. Maybe their lifeboat would hit an iceberg, too, and sink.

"Mama," piped up a child, "where will we go to bed?"

"We'll wait for a ship," his mother answered. "It will come and pick us up and we'll all go to bed on our rescue ship."

"But when will the ship come?" the child asked. "I'm sleepy *now*." His voice brightened and he asked, "Will the *Titanic* come back for us, Mama?"

The reassuring voice faltered this time. "No, Ned. No. Just lean against me and close your eyes. It's late, and the *Titanic* won't be coming back."

CHAPTER 11

The Longest Night
Monday, April 15, 1912, 2:45 A.M.

The world had shrunk to the size of Lifeboat Number 4.

The *Titanic* was gone. And the people.

Surely they weren't all gone. Not all of them. Not Mr. Daniel. Not Finn.

Not Mr. Kingsbury. Not Bucky. *Bucky.*

Green flares occasionally shot up from other lifeboats, so somebody else had to be out there with them.

Sam pressed his arms around Star's chest, seeking warmth. His head throbbed and a crust of dried blood had formed over his eye, where he'd hit his head earlier. Mr. Hemmings had wrung out his flat wool cap. It was still damp, but he pulled it down over Sam's head so that even his ears were covered. It helped. His eyes were adjusted to the darkness now, and he recognized a figure his own size, across from him on the next bench. It was Willie Carter, the boy who'd owned the King Charles spaniels. Willie was wearing a lady's wide-brimmed velvet hat with a huge feather plume draped across the top. Sam couldn't help smiling at the sight of it. It made Willie look like a girl.

"Don't plague me with squirming, Ned," the mother seated on the bottom of the lifeboat snapped. "Lean against me and try to get some sleep."

"But I'm cold, Mama," Ned wailed.

Sam shivered, and Hemmings reached out and put a comforting hand on his shoulder. For the first time, Sam realized he wasn't just shivering. He was also whimpering, and he couldn't stop. He felt so empty inside. So alone.

Hemmings started to hum. Then he sang in a deep baritone voice: "Old maids say I have no sense, Boys declare I'm just immense, Though fond of fun, I'm never rude, Though not too bad, I'm not too good."

"Stop singing," Perkis commanded. "This is hardly the time or place for it."

"It's exactly the time and place," Mrs. Astor shot back at him. "Sometimes it's necessary to sing in order to . . ." Her voice quavered. "In order to know you're still alive."

"Come on, folks! It'll warm you," Hemmings

urged. "You all know the chorus. Ta-ra-ra-boom-de-ay, Ta-ra-ra-boom-de-ay, Ta-ra-ra-boom-de-ay, Ta-ra-ra-boom-de-ay!"

Several women joined in halfheartedly, rousing enough to take the old song through another round of *ta-ra-ra*s. Sam opened his mouth to join in. Bucky would want him to sing along. But the words stuck in his throat, and he started to hiccup as warm, wet tears rolled down his cheeks.

Over the course of the next few hours, they tied up with four other lifeboats, making a sort of roped-together raft.

Besides their own boat, there were Lifeboats 10, 12, 14, and Collapsible D. Perkis had "ceded command" to Officer Lowe in Lifeboat 14. Now they had a lantern, and there was more talk about when a rescue ship would come.

But the night dragged on.

Sam and Hemmings huddled up against each other, with Star across their laps like a steamer rug.

Sam leaned against the gunwale, staring over the side at the small white cakes of ice that milled through the water. The last time he'd felt this cold was the night in late March when his father died. It was snowing that night as if it would never stop. Sam had stood outside the closed window in the snow, not able to go inside the house because his father was quarantined. He'd never even been able to say good-bye to him face-to-face. Now all he had left of his father were memories, and all he knew of his mother came from her letters.

Sam had managed to sneak some of those letters into his trunk, despite what Gramp said. He had crammed them into a five-pound flour tin.

Sam had planned to throw those letters, fistfuls at a time, right in the faces of his mother and Jack. Then he'd run far away where no one could ever find him.

Sam laid his head on his arm and closed his eyes. He couldn't do that now. The letters, his trunk, his coat, his good shoes, everything except Star had gone down with the *Titanic*.

A growler, a tiny iceberg about the size of Gramp's padded footstool, kept bumping against the side of the boat in a monotonous rhythm. Sam kept his eyes closed, trying to sleep, but each bump reawakened him. It bumped them again and again. He would go mad if that growler touched them one more time.

Bump. He wished he had an ax to chop it up into tiny pieces. *Bump.*

Star began to bark, an insistent warning bark.

"Keep that mutt quiet," Perkis growled.

In the next moment, the piercing sound of a whistle split the morning air.

The horizon glowed with the promise of a rising sun, and the icebergs, some nearly as tall as the *Titanic* herself had been, floated around them like ghostly giants. The whistle blasted, then blasted again.

The whistling was coming from a ship. It was a much smaller ship than the *Titanic,* but from the lifeboat, it looked huge.

Officer Lowe ordered the ropes untied, and Lifeboat Number 10 and Collapsible D started toward the rescue ship. From behind him, Sam heard faint, distant voices, shouting. He blinked, wondering if he was already seeing ghosts. It looked like a group of men from the *Titanic* were standing on the water.

Sam rubbed his eyes and squinted. There were two rows of men in neat lines, leaning first one way and then the other. An officer stood in front of the lines, blowing a whistle to signal the shifts. The men were standing on something round and long.

"Are they standing on an iceberg?" Hemmings asked. He, too, was peering over the gunwale at the strange sight. "Maybe it's a really big growler."

"They're standing on an overturned collapsible!" Lowe yelled. "Let's get them!"

"Yeah! An upside-down collapsible lifeboat," agreed Hemmings. "They have canvas sides that have to be popped into place and locked. From the looks of it, this one didn't pop." He whistled softly under his breath. "Those men are the lucky ones, to still make use of that boat."

"*Lucky* isn't a word that fits anything about this day," Mrs. Astor whispered bitterly.

"If you please, Miss," Hemmings answered her gently. "It's always a lucky day if a body's alive to see it."

"Come on now, pull!" Perkis shouted. "Put your backs into it, people."

It was hard to believe the quartermaster, who would have been sweeping the hat off his head for these ladies just a few hours ago, was now ordering them to row. Sam grabbed an oar, along with Hemmings and Mrs. Astor, and the three of them, working with the others, strained to move the clumsy lifeboat through the slate gray water.

The men on the overturned collapsible seemed miles away.

"Come over and take us on!" hailed the officer with the whistle.

"Aye, aye, Mr. Lightoller, sir," Hemmings called back.

A wash of waves crested over the bobbing plat-form. The breeze was picking up, and the men looked like tightrope walkers, testing their balance. Sam spotted Colonel Gracie, his mustache covered with tiny icicles.

Perkis clumsily maneuvered their lifeboat alongside the collapsible.

"No rocking the boat," said Lightoller sternly. "Don't scramble off, boys. We'll take this gently, one at a time."

Even so, the collapsible gave a sickening roll as the first man leaned forward to jump. But one after the other, they all leaped to the safety of Lifeboats Number 4 and 12.

The women were already asking the men from the collapsible for news of their husbands, but the newcomers knew no more than they did. Sam shouted to Colonel Gracie, but the man didn't turn to look at him. He didn't seem to hear him.

A starburst of white light lit up the gray sky, and everyone cheered and applauded. It was a rocket fired by the approaching steamship. Sam could just make out the name on the side of the ship—*Carpathia*.

A line of faces stared down at them from *Carpathia*'s promenade deck. Perkis grabbed at the rope netting along the big ship's side as they drew abreast.

"Where's my son? Where's my boy?" yelled a frantic voice from above them, and Sam bent his neck and looked up into the worried face of a man leaning far over *Carpathia*'s rail.

"Here I am, Father." Willie Carter lifted the wide-brimmed lady's hat he still had on his head. "I'm right here."

"Thank God!" Mr. Carter cried. "Everything's all right, Willie. You'll be on board in no time."

It was true. Rescue was at hand. But everything would never be "all right" again.

CHAPTER 12

On the *Carpathia*

Monday, April 15, 1912, 6:30 A.M.

Once Sam was aboard, the first person he recognized on *Carpathia*'s deck was Mr. Ismay. Ismay stood with his back against the rail, his face white and sunken like a skull. His mustache looked quite black and full against it. There was another man standing beside him, arguing with him about something, but Mr. Ismay was only shaking his head.

Sam grabbed Star and walked toward the pair. Along the way, someone wrapped Sam in a dry blanket and pressed a steaming mug of hot cider into his hands. Even though he was exhausted, Sam knew it would be better to get this over with right away, to let Mr. Ismay know his dog was all right.

"Won't you go into the salon? It's warm in there," a gentleman was urging Ismay.

"I don't want anything."

"You must go and eat something hot to warm you up. Why, you're trembling with cold and shock. I'm the ship's doctor, and it's clear to me that you—"

"If you would leave me be, I would be most grateful," Ismay interrupted him. "Just give me a quiet room where I can be alone."

"Please," the doctor said, "go to the salon."

"I would rather not."

"Mr. Ismay," Sam began. "Mr. Ismay, I have your—"

But before Sam could get another word out, the doctor was shushing him and shooing him away. "Best not to bother this man with anything right now, son. I fear he's unwell."

The doctor took Ismay's elbow and led him toward the entrance to the officers' quarters. "I'm going to put you in my cabin," he told Ismay in a low voice. "Don't worry about a thing. You're safe now. That's all that matters."

Sam stared after them. Mr. Ismay hadn't even glanced at Star. The dog leaned against Sam's legs, gazing up at him. The longer Sam kept Star, the harder it was going to be to give him back.

Sam sighed and looked around at the small crowd of survivors, many of whom stared vacantly back at him. Where was Bucky? and Lady Cabot? and Robert Daniel? and Finn?

Where was Bucky?

Sam kept glancing out over the rail at the water studded with icebergs glowing pink in the early morning light. More boats would appear any minute. If they just waited a little longer. If they looked a little harder.

Sam's mug of cider was losing its steam in the cold air. He raised the lukewarm brown liquid to his lips and took a sip.

But he couldn't swallow. Tears came, silent and choking, and he had to spit his mouthful of cider over the rail.

"Are you all right?" came a calm voice behind Sam. A thin man holding a pencil stub and a sheaf of ship's stationery bent down to pat Star. "My name is Carlos Hurd and I'm a passenger on the *Carpathia*. Is there anything I can do to help?"

"Do you have another pencil and some paper I could borrow?" Sam asked.

Hurd smiled at him. "We'll get you into some drier clothes too. Come on, son. Let's see what we can find." He took off his jacket and draped it around Sam's shoulders.

Carlos Hurd turned out to be a reporter for the *St. Louis Post-Dispatch* in Missouri. Mr. Hurd had been on his way to the Mediterranean for vacation, but now he was trying to collect stories for the *New York World,* whose editor was a friend of his.

"Here, Sam. The clothes will be too big for you, but they're warm and dry," Mr. Hurd said as he pulled some clothes and paper out of the trunk in his room. "Reporters from the *World* will be waiting when the *Carpathia* docks in New York, and I'm going to give them the biggest story of any reporter's lifetime."

"But Mr. Hurd," Sam said, "didn't *Carpathia*'s Captain Rostron say survivors shouldn't be disturbed with questions?"

Mr. Hurd handed the paper to Sam. "This is history, son. We're not letting it sink with *Titanic.* Someday people will want to know what happened, every detail, horrible as it was. They'll look to the papers for answers."

"My dad was a reporter," Sam said quietly.

"Then you know the value of the written word."

"Yes sir," Sam said. "Can I help you collect stories?"

Mr. Hurd laid a hand on Sam's shoulder. "Are you sure you are up to that? It's not going to be easy, son."

"I need to do something," Sam said.

Mr. Hurd nodded. "All right. We'll get started tomorrow. For now, you try to rest."

The rest of the first day on the *Carpathia* passed in a blur. There was a service for the missing, presided over by Captain Rostron. It took forever to hitch the empty lifeboats onto *Carpathia*'s decks, and even then, some were left floating empty on the ocean swells. Another ship came and took over the hunt for survivors. By noontime, the *Carpathia* was steaming slowly through the ice field, heading for New York. It was like a toy ship compared to the *Titanic*. It had only one funnel instead of four, and now passengers were crammed into every inch of all the cabins and public rooms.

For such a crowded ship, it was amazingly quiet. People spoke in whispers. There was no music. No dancing. No laughter.

Sam was glad to come upon Lady Cabot wandering aimlessly on the promenade deck. The moment she saw him, she threw her arms around him and sobbed into his shoulder. She asked him if he'd seen Colonel Gracie. He told her the colonel had been rescued from Collapsible B and had to be aboard somewhere. He asked her if she'd seen Bucky.

She didn't answer.

She clung to Sam for a long time before looking him up and down. "What do you have on your feet?" She frowned. "Where are your good shoes?"

"I lost them. In the water."

"What am I to do with a boy who can't even hold on to his . . ." Her scolding voice faltered. "Who loses his best . . ."

"Friend?" Sam whispered. Tears ran down his cheeks again.

"Oh, Sam," Lady Cabot whispered. "It was such a horrible night." She walked him over to an empty deck chair and pulled him onto her lap. Then she rocked him and crooned softly. It was an old lullaby of his grandmum's that Sam almost remembered. He liked the sound of it.

In fact, he preferred Lady Cabot's soft singing to the stony silence of Bucky's mother that afternoon. At first, when Lady Cabot brought Mrs. Kingsbury to see him, she only stared at him.

"*You're* alive?" she finally asked. "Where is my Buckthorn?" Her voice was accusing. "He was *always* with you. You and that dog. You still have that dog." Her voice was becoming shrill. "Where is Buckthorn? His father said they'd be along. He promised me. And you're here. So where are *they*?"

She swayed on her feet, and only Lady Cabot's steadying arm kept her upright. "Shush now," Lady Cabot whispered, and led the sobbing Mrs. Kingsbury away.

Later that day Sam discovered Robert Daniel on board, staring in silence out at the water. Sam ran to him and grabbed his hand, pumping it up and down.

"Mr. Daniel, you're alive! And Pye? Where's Pye?" Sam asked. His friend continued to stare out at the endless sweep of gray water. "Mr. Daniel?"

"Pye is gone." Robert Daniel's voice was matter-of-fact, like the voice of a banker reading a column of numbers. "I had him in my arms, Sam. I put him in a life vest, just the way you suggested. The ship was almost gone when we jumped. It was jump or be sucked under. There wasn't any choice. But when I bobbed up to the surface, I only had the life jacket in my arms. It was too big for Pye. I knew it, but I thought I could hold on. And when the chance came to get into a lifeboat . . ." Robert Daniel's voice broke on the last two words.

He looked down at Star and knelt in front of the dog, stroking Star's fur slowly. Star didn't prance or bounce or try to lick. He stood completely still for Mr. Daniel now.

"That young man who plays tennis . . ." Mr. Daniel paused. "I can't recall his name. But he got himself into the half-opened collapsible with us." Mr. Daniel smiled as if he almost found the image funny—a collapsible already half collapsed. "He said he saw Pye in the water. He figured I'd gone down for sure then, because Pye was never anywhere without me."

Mr. Daniel looked up at Sam, his eyes glistening. "His pups would have made the finest line of French bulldogs America ever saw, Sam. I'm sure of it. But there'll never be another dog like Pye."

Carlos Hurd had come up behind Sam and was silently scribbling notes on a pad of paper.

Sam asked, hearing the slight tremble in his own voice, "Did you see Miss Isham, Mr. Daniel? Did she get on a boat?"

Robert Daniel shook his head. "I didn't see her. But she would never leave Toujours behind. He was her family. She'd raised that dog from a pup, all those years she lived in Paris."

Mr. Daniel looked out over the water again, staring at nothing. "How could we leave them all? So many souls lost, and we're still here. That's all we have, Sam. 'Hows' and 'whys' and 'what ifs.'" Mr. Daniel stood up suddenly and walked away from Sam and Star, stomping angrily down the deck.

Sam felt Mr. Hurd's hand on his shoulder. "He's not mad at you, lad. I think he may be mad at God Himself, and I can't say as I blame him. A lot of the folks we've been talking to feel the same way."

Mr. Hurd lowered his voice. "But keep our little interviews under your hat. Captain Rostron won't let me send any telegrams ahead. He doesn't want any news getting out before we dock. But we'll get our chance to tell the story the way it should be told." Sam couldn't think of a way the story could be told. At least not a way that didn't hurt.

"It would help if you'd jot down the story your friend just told you about his dog." Mr. Hurd paused. "Do you feel up to it, Sam?"

Sam nodded. He couldn't look up at Mr. Hurd. Not when he could feel the warm tears spilling down his cheeks.

Pye gone. Finn gone.

Bucky gone.

Sam gathered Star into his arms as Mr. Hurd walked away. He buried his face in the dog's coat.

It wasn't fair. The thought drummed inside his head and wouldn't shut up. It wasn't fair.

CHAPTER 13

Surviving

Tuesday, April 16, 1912

The world was still as upside down as when Sam and Star first hit that icy water.

After a night on the floor of *Carpathia*'s dining room, Sam awoke groggily to the smell of coffee and cinnamon rolls. Busy stewards carried trays and plates to tables that were already filling up with passengers. Star hovered over Sam, his front legs spread apart like a guard on duty, giving little muffled growls if any steward's foot got too close to Sam.

"I think you'll be stepped on soon, despite your vigilant companion, if you don't move," came a voice from overhead.

Sam looked at a pair of black lace-up leather shoes, then up into the smiling face of Carlos Hurd. Mr. Hurd pulled his jacket open just wide enough for Sam to see the edge of a pad of paper and the sharpened end of a pencil in his inside pocket.

"We're getting close to New York," Hurd said. Then he leaned over and whispered, "We still have work to do."

"I'll be right there," Sam assured him. "As soon as I get Star walked."

At the word *walk*, Star jumped and yipped happily.

Mr. Hurd grinned. "From the looks of it, that dog's going to take *you* for a walk. Not the other way around."

Star lunged for a steward passing with a tray of bacon. Sam grabbed his collar just in time. The steward frowned and held his tray as far away from the dog as possible. Star's eyes stayed glued to the steaming bacon as it disappeared across the room. Sam produced the piece he had snatched from the tray and gave it to Star, who wolfed it down in one bite.

"You might want to clean yourself up a bit, lad," Hurd urged. "Do you want me to find you better clothes? You're looking a bit like"—Hurd paused and grinned wryly—"like a survivor from a shipwreck."

The words made Sam smile, too, but only for an instant. "I'd really rather stay the way I am, if you don't mind." He stood up and tried to shake some of the wrinkles out of the oversize white shirt and dark pants

Mr. Hurd had given him. Without the borrowed belt, notched several inches in with the help of a penknife, the pants would have fallen down.

It made Sam feel better to look so awful. Other survivors clearly felt the same way, not combing their hair or changing their clothes.

As Sam and Mr. Hurd found out through quiet, patient questioning of *Titanic*'s survivors, only three *Titanic* dogs, besides Star, were aboard the *Carpathia:* Elizabeth Rothschild's yappy little Pomeranian; Margaret Hays's sweetly patient Pom, who had become the primary comfort of Lolo and Momon, the newly orphaned French boys whose care Miss Hayes had undertaken; and Henry Sleeper Harper's imperial Pekingese, Sun Yat-Sen, carried everywhere by the silent Egyptian dragoman who was accompanying Harper back to America. Harper, his servant, and his dog had all boarded Lifeboat Number 3. Harper said there'd been room for more in the boat, but no one else was willing to board before it was lowered.

Sam shuddered at the memory of little Frou-Frou's frantic barking, locked in her B-deck cabin. Locked there forever.

He tried to remember all of *Titanic*'s dogs. The big chow had a coat thick enough to keep it warm at the North Pole. Perhaps it had climbed out onto an iceberg and was, even now, trying to dig out a warm den. The little fox terrier could have hitched a ride on the chow's back and ridden to safety. Sam liked imagining the pair safe and warm together. He'd told Mr. Hurd about Madeleine Astor seeing her Airedale, Kitty, on deck with her husband, just before the *Titanic* sank. But Mrs. Astor didn't want to talk to them about it.

By the end of two days, Sam and Mr. Hurd had collected piles of handwritten accounts.

"These are incredible!" Mr. Hurd exclaimed to his wife, Catherine.

"And heartbreaking," added Mrs. Hurd. "Sam, I do wish you'd share our cabin with us. You look exhausted from sleeping on that dining room floor."

"I'm all right," Sam said. "I like to sleep next to Star. Besides, Lady Cabot is already having fits because I won't sleep on the floor of her cabin. But the woman she's sharing with doesn't like dogs."

A knock on the door made all three of them jump.

"Mr. Hurd, we've been ordered to search your cabin," a voice boomed from outside. "Please open the door!"

"What should we do?" Sam whispered fearfully. "Maybe they'll go away if we don't make any noise."

The knocking came again, louder and more insistent. Star growled, low in his throat, and began to bark.

Mrs. Hurd quickly stacked the papers on a chair

and sat on them, spreading her long skirt over them. "Open the door, Carlos," she said.

The officer frowned as he entered the room. "Mr. Hurd, we've received word that you're collecting stories." His eyes scanned the room until they settled on a corner of paper peeking out from under Mrs. Hurd's dress. The officer blinked, took off his cap, and scratched his neatly parted hair.

"Well, find anything?" Mr. Hurd demanded. "You realize, of course, that a search like this is unconstitutional and could result in courtroom prosecution of you and Captain Rostron and the whole Cunard line?"

The officer backed quickly to the door. "If the lady would stand . . ." He stopped and cleared his throat, his face turning red. "No sir, didn't find anything. Good day."

He shut the door just before Sam burst out laughing.

"That's the only time good manners have ever worked in my favor as a reporter," Mr. Hurd said.

But Sam's smile faded quickly when he returned to the grim silence on deck. The strange thing was, it was hard not to feel guilty about surviving. Sam couldn't shake the feeling he had done something wrong by just being alive.

CHAPTER 14

New York Harbor
Thursday, April 18, 1912

Rain fell as the *Carpathia* steamed into the mouth of
New York harbor. Distant voices shouted from a mass of
circling tugboats, where flashbulbs dotted the darkness
with small bursts of light.

"No reporters," Captain Rostron warned his crew.
"If anyone tries to come aboard before we dock, confine
them immediately."

Carlos Hurd paced the promenade deck, an oilskin
package clutched to his chest. Inside was a cigar box
filled with wine corks nestled around pages and pages of
handwritten accounts from several dozen *Titanic* survivors. The accounts had been gathered in secret, but
the *Carpathia* was abuzz with Hurd's project.

Having the pages, however, and getting them to the *New York World* were two entirely different things.

Sam followed Hurd as he paced.

Star followed Sam.

Like a small parade, man, boy, and dog circled the deck, looking for a way to pass the precious papers to the *World*'s tugboat. It was out there somewhere, chugging along in that covey of tugboats gathering like squat little ducklings on all sides of the *Carpathia*. Finding it wouldn't be easy.

Banners were draped across the pilot cabin of a nearby tugboat. TELL US YOUR STORY, it said, WE'LL PAY. Men with megaphones yelled booming questions at the people on *Carpathia*, but Sam could hear only snippets of what was being asked.

"Is Mrs. Astor . . ."

". . . hear the captain's final words before . . ."

". . . true about Major Butt?"

No answers were shouted back. No one really had any answers.

"We're in the Ambrose Channel," Hurd shouted into Sam's ear. It was hard to hear over the din. "We're slowing to pick up a pilot. He'll help guide us into New York City Harbor."

Heads craned over the side as a pilot began his

climb up the rope ladder. Several reporters were trying to push their way aboard right behind him, but Captain Rostron had the ladder pulled up as the pilot climbed. One stout reporter jumped to catch the dangling end of the rope and splashed feetfirst into the water.

Dusk had passed into nighttime as the *Carpathia* steamed into the lower harbor, slowing again at the quarantine stop on the Twelfth Street dock. One of the tugboats bumped into the ship's side. Above the general jumble of shouts, Sam could make out a name being called. "Hurd."

"Down there!" Sam urged. "They're calling your name from down there."

Sure enough. "Here, Hurd! Throw it here! We're from the *World!* Throw it to us!"

Mr. Hurd leaned far out over the rail, then quickly straightened up and grinned at Sam. "It's Charles Chapin, the editor of the *World*. That's the very boat, the *Dalzelline*."

Mr. Hurd handed the package to Sam, who climbed atop the rail, holding on to a stanchion with one hand and waving his parcel with the other.

"Here! Over here!" Sam yelled. "This is from Carlos Hurd. Are you ready?"

Sam's arm curled back, and he heaved the tightly

wrapped bundle of pages toward the waiting boat. A momentary hush fell as Sam and the crowd that had gathered behind him watched the shiny oilskin glisten with reflected light as it dropped down, and down, and—

Sam gasped. The precious package snagged on a lifeboat line and swung there, just out of reach of the *Dalzelline*.

"Get that thing!" Captain Rostron shouted, and a sailor swung out over the rail and jiggled the line vigorously. "Bring it to me," Rostron commanded, but the parcel came loose and plummeted down the side of the ship, right into the waiting arms of a man on the *Dalzelline*.

With several toots of its whistle, the boat pushed away from the *Carpathia* and steamed for shore, the true story of the *Titanic* disaster safely carried to the presses of the *New York World*.

Sam climbed down beside Star, putting his arms around the dog. Now everyone would hear what had happened. It wouldn't matter in the end. Not any of it. Unless another ship was coming in behind them with more survivors, there'd be no Bucky, and no more survivor stories left to tell.

Sam pulled Star over against the wall of the first-class smoking room on the promenade deck, out of the way of the milling throng.

"Sam?" Lady Cabot's voice came from above his head, and he looked up into her pale face. "We'll be docking soon, and I must see you properly delivered to your mother."

"Now?" Sam asked, remembering that his mother was still married to a stranger. Star would still have to go back to Mr. Ismay.

"Soon." Lady Cabot's voice was a husky whisper and she dabbed at her eyes with a crumpled lace kerchief. Her usually neat bun hung lopsided, and her clothes, like Sam's, were a strange collection—a red blouse from the trunk of one *Carpathia* passenger and a full blue-checked skirt from the trunk of another. She wore only the broach and earrings she'd worn getting into the lifeboat. No bracelets. None of her beloved pearl necklaces. All of those were in a round red leather box at the bottom of the North Atlantic.

"Ah, there you are, my boy!" Mr. Hurd came over and lifted his hat to Lady Cabot. "I wanted to give you this, Sam."

Hurd placed a sleek black-and-gold fountain pen into Sam's hand. "Just a small token of appreciation for your help. You'll make a fine newspaperman someday."

"Thank you, sir." Sam slipped the pen into his

pocket and looked down at his feet. He couldn't say good-bye. He'd said good-bye to too many people already.

Mr. Hurd squeezed Sam's shoulder and bent down to ruffle the fur between Star's ears. "We'll meet again someday, Sam. I hope you know that if there were any way to fix it so this dog could be yours, I'd do it. But I know you're strong enough to take whatever comes. You've proved that. You're going to be fine."

Sam didn't believe it, but he nodded in mute agreement.

"Catherine and I have to go below and finish packing." Hurd was already turning away. "I'll write to you, Sam," he called back. "And don't forget to buy the *World* tomorrow morning. We'll be all over the front page."

"What time is it?" Lady Cabot asked a passing gentleman.

He pulled out his pocket watch and flipped it open. "It's nearly nine-thirty. We should be disembarking shortly now that we've docked."

This was it, then.

They were home.

Sam looked down at Star. He should try to find Mr. Ismay before he left the *Carpathia*. He couldn't just walk away with a valuable dog that didn't belong to him.

A sea of people lined the dock below. They spoke

in hushed tones as if they were in church. A steady drizzle fell through the glow of the lamps that lined the pier. Sam leaned down and took Star's head in his hands. "I don't know what to do, boy. What are we going to do?"

Star's tail, its tip hanging at half-mast, beat sympathetically against the deck.

CHAPTER 15

In His Mother's Arms

Thursday, April 18, 1912

Sam waited with Star by the rail of the promenade deck as a steady stream of passengers walked past. Two women strolled by, locked in conversation.

"... shameful, shameful behavior. Why, I shan't be surprised to learn the man saved his own steamer trunk. Dear Frank and Edward are missing and here's the *president* of the steamship line, walking around fine as you please.

"One more word protesting his innocence from that Ismay, and I shall scream. It's just too, too cowardly that a man should . . ."

Sam couldn't hear the rest. They had walked out of earshot.

Sam concentrated on the next group coming down

the deck toward him. A gentleman in livery carried the sleeping figure of a small boy in his arms. A young woman carried a second boy while a Pomeranian trotted down the deck beside them.

The lady said something in French to the boy in her arms.

This had to be Miss Margaret Hayes and the two little French boys she'd taken charge of. The young orphans didn't seem to have a mother or father, or speak any English, or even know their own last names. A man had simply plopped them down in the last lifeboat and kissed them good-bye. No one knew quite what to do with them until Miss Hayes, who spoke fluent French, took over.

Miss Hayes's little dog paused beside Star and tilted its head up to touch noses. Miss Hayes looked down. "Ah," she whispered to Sam. "The boy who saved the big dog. Good luck."

"Those look like deep thoughts you're having, son," came a voice behind him, and Sam swung his head around to see Robert Daniel. "Steady there." Mr. Daniel laid his hand on Sam's shoulder. "Well, we made the trip of a lifetime, wouldn't you say? Though this isn't quite the way I pictured myself arriving in New York."

He wore a battered derby with a hole in the crown, and his pants were a good two inches too short. An inch of white long johns showed beneath their hem. Around his shoulders, a plaid steamer rug was fastened like a shawl.

"You look fine to me," Sam said, but he couldn't keep his face from breaking into a grin.

"Well, you look as if it'll take you at least three more years to grow into those clothes you're wearing," Mr. Daniel shot back. "You make a pair, you and that crook-tailed dog." Star licked Mr. Daniel's hands as he scratched the furry ruff of his chest.

"I'm waiting to see Mr. Ismay about Star." Sam watched as Lady Cabot came toward them with Captain Rostron in tow.

"This is Sam Harris," she explained to the captain. "He's trying to do the right thing by this dog, but we can't keep waiting here for Mr. Ismay forever."

Captain Rostron shook Sam's hand. He looked down at Star. "I have to tell you, son, Mr. Ismay has refused all visitors. He's not eating or sleeping and barely says a word. In fact, he's still under the care of our ship's doctor. I'm afraid there'll be no chance for you to talk to him tonight. But you might find him at the Senate inquiry at the Waldorf-Astoria tomorrow. Why don't you take the dog with you? That's the best advice I can give you."

"But Star . . . ," Sam began.

". . . will come with us," finished Mr. Daniel.

"Good luck, Master Harris," Captain Rostron called after them as they headed down the deck.

Robert Daniel propelled Sam off the ship and into the crowd of people on the pier. Reporters surged forward, surrounding them. Mr. Daniel took their questions and motioned for Sam and Lady Cabot to push ahead.

While Sam and Lady Cabot threaded their way between hundreds of people, Sam searched the faces.

Then he heard her.

"Sammy! Oh, Sam! Here! We're over here!" called an achingly familiar voice.

A path in the crowd cleared between Sam and the open arms of a woman in a broad-brimmed, brown velvet hat.

Sam wasn't aware of dropping Star's lead. He wasn't aware of running. All he knew was, in the time it took his eyes to blink at the sight of her, he was in his mother's arms. He buried his face in the soft wool of her coat and breathed in the familiar smell of her lilac cologne.

His mother was talking, hugging him, rocking him. "My poor Sam. There was a theatrical producer named Harris onboard the *Titanic*, and at first they said there was a 'Boy Harris' saved, but they didn't think it was you. They thought it was *his* son. Jack and I didn't know if you were even . . . Oh, Sam!"

Another arm went around Sam's shoulder, and the scent of fresh lime shaving cream mixed with his mother's lilac. It was Jack. It was the man Sam hadn't wanted to meet. He was embracing them both in strong arms. "Your mother never gave up hope, Sam," Jack said.

Sam closed his eyes, resting in his mother's arms. He had planned to be angry with her. He had convinced himself he didn't need her or anyone else before the sinking. But he wanted her now, more than he'd ever thought possible.

"Will you be all right, Samuel?" Lady Cabot had been joined by several of her friends. "Do you need me to stay?"

Sam shook his head. He didn't trust his voice.

Lady Cabot hugged him tightly.

"Thank you, Lavinia. Thank you for bringing him safely back to us," Sam's mother said. Lady Cabot nodded, and then her friends wrapped her in a blanket and hurried her to a waiting hansom cab.

"So, Sam, who's your friend?" Jack dropped to one knee and ran practiced hands over Star's deep chest and legs. The hands paused for only a second when they came to the bend in Star's feathery tail. Jack's face tilted up, his blue-gray eyes looking directly at Sam. "This is one fine dog, even with that notch in his tail."

"He's not mine." Sam said the words so low, he could barely hear them himself. But Jack nodded.

"Whoever he belongs to, Sam, it's clear *he* thinks he's yours, and, for tonight, that's good enough."

"But, Jack . . . ," Sam's mother started.

Jack shook his head, stood, and began to guide all three of them toward a line of waiting carriages. "We'll sort it all out tomorrow, Sarah. It's way too late to worry about it tonight."

"But . . . ," his mother began again, "what if the hotel won't take dogs?"

Panting, Mr. Daniel caught up with them, grabbing Sam's arm. "I just heard the Madison Hotel will take *any* survivor of the *Titanic* disaster, free of charge! Star qualifies as a survivor as much as the rest of us!"

Mr. Daniel tilted his derby to Sam's mother and shook Jack's hand. "Take care of Sam," he told them.

He took Sam's hand and shook it firmly. "You're a good man, Sam. A good friend. I hope you'll write me." He slipped a scribbled address into Sam's hand. "I promise I'll write back. I'll need your advice about the new kennel I plan to open. 'The Gamin de Pycombe Memorial Home for Dogs.' Sounds good, doesn't it?"

Then Robert Daniel was gone, too.

Jack loaded them into a cab, and Sam ended up in the middle with Star between his legs. He leaned back against the tufted leather seat, the rhythm of the cab's jouncing and the clip-clopping of the horse's hooves lulling him to sleep. He didn't even notice his head leaning against Jack's solid shoulder.

CHAPTER 16

A Guiding Star

Friday, April 19, 1912

They were the only ones. The survivors picked up by the *Carpathia* were the only survivors. The *New York Globe*, the *Times*, and all the other papers carried lists in their morning editions. No other ships pulled into New York harbor carrying survivors. No more heartfelt reunions unfolded on the docks between the rescued and their waiting families. All that was left were names on a list. They didn't use the words *lived* or *died*. Beside each name was printed *Saved* or *Lost*.

Sam Harris	Saved
Ann Isham	Lost
Buckthorn Kingsbury III	Lost

| Webb Kingsbury | Lost |
| Phineas MacDougal | Lost |

Sam threw the whole stack of newspapers down on the table in the sitting room of their hotel suite.

Jack picked them up, flipping through the pages. "Quite a story here about a Newfoundland dog named Rigel that saved Lifeboat Number 4."

"What?" Sam jumped up and tore the paper out of Jack's hands. "There was no Newfoundland on the *Titanic*. That's just crazy."

"Then I guess it's true that you can't believe everything you read in the papers," Jack said mildly. "You were in Lifeboat Number 4, weren't you?"

Sam nodded.

"No heroic dog in the water at all?"

"Just Star."

"Well, I don't know where this dining room steward from the *Carpathia* got his Rigel story, but with newspapers offering to pay people for a good survivor yarn, it was bound to happen that some people would start making things up."

Every newspaper in the city was full of stories. Some of them, Sam barely remembered. Lots of others, he didn't believe: People shot by *Titanic*'s crew as they fought to get on lifeboats? Men dressing up as women to sneak to safety?

Sam had seen none of that.

He had, however, heard *Titanic*'s band playing until the very moment the lights blinked out and the ship upended. He'd seen the elderly Ida and Isidor Straus, the rich owners of Macy's department store, give up their seats on a lifeboat to young people. He'd seen the men who somehow stayed alive balancing on the bottom of an overturned lifeboat, working together to stay afloat.

Sam read every story with the by-line "Carlos Hurd." At least *those* stories were true.

"Looks to me like Star can't be a show dog anymore," Jack commented as he salted the scrambled eggs room service had brought. "You can't show a dog with a broken tail."

Sam looked down at Star curled at his feet. "How do *you* know Star can't be a show dog?" Sam challenged.

Jack put down his paper and stared at Sam. "Didn't your mother ever tell you how I make my living?"

Sam shook his head.

"We have a lot to learn about each other, Sam. I'm a veterinarian. I've got a practice in Bucks County, Pennsylvania, and a few of my clients are show dogs.

That's how I know how strict those ring judges can be. See here?"

Jack bent down and snapped his fingers. Star stood up, stretched, and trotted over to him and put a paw on his knee. Jack ran a gentle hand over Star's back and tail. "Even if this tail were to be rebroken and set, it would leave a scar—a lump, actually. That would be seen as a flaw in the show ring." Jack ruffled his fingers through Star's thick fur and scratched his muzzle. Star stretched out his head in blissful contentment.

"Star's perfect, from head to tail."

"He's a fine dog," Jack agreed. "Just not show dog material anymore."

"Do you think Mr. Ismay will blame me for his broken tail?" Sam asked.

"I think Mr. Ismay is lucky to have his dog alive at all, and he has you to thank for it, Sam. You saved this animal's life."

Sam felt a blush inching up his neck. He looked down at his new shoes. His mother had already been out shopping that morning, so he'd have "something decent" to wear. She'd gone to a special "survivor's sale" at Macy's department store.

Sam finally looked up again and met Jack's eyes. "Star saved *my* life. I didn't save his."

Jack nodded and leaned forward, studying Sam. "The question is, what do you want to do about Star now?"

"I have to give him back, don't I?" Sam's voice sounded as miserable as the rest of him felt.

"What do you think you *should* do, Sam?" asked Jack.

Sam slid out of his chair and onto the floor. Star drew close and laid his head in Sam's lap. "I guess his broken tail wouldn't stop him from being in advertisements and brochures for the White Star Line. Would it?"

"I don't know," Jack mused. "I'm not sure how much promotion the White Star Line will be doing for a spell. They're not going to want people to remember the *Titanic,* and Star was a dog on the *Titanic.* That could be a problem for the line."

"What do *you* think I should do?" Sam asked.

"Well, Sam, a man has to do what's right. The hard part is usually figuring out what that is."

"Maybe Mr. Ismay has already gone back to England." Sam's voice was hopeful. "Maybe he's forgotten about Star."

Jack picked up a paper from the pile on the table. He pointed to a front-page headline: ISMAY TO TESTIFY TODAY AT THE WALDORF-ASTORIA.

Sam sighed, pulled Star's lead out of his pocket, and clipped it to the dog's collar. "I want to get it over with," he told Jack. "Can you tell me how to get to the Waldorf-Astoria?"

"Would you mind if I came along?" Jack asked.

Sam nodded. "Suit yourself." But he was secretly glad for Jack's company.

They walked from the Madison Hotel, stopping to read the chalked-up bulletins above the White Star offices: ISMAY TESTIFIES. SENATOR SMITH ASKS HOW SUCH A TRAGEDY COULD HAPPEN.

Sam still had what sailors called sea legs, and he lurched a bit as he walked, as if he expected the sidewalk to rear up in front of him at any minute. He walked slowly, letting Star's leash hang limp in his hand. The longer it took to get there, the longer he and Star would be together.

Star crowded close to Sam's legs. He kept lifting his head to look at Sam, whining softly.

The flags at the hotel's entrance flew at half-mast in honor of Waldorf-Astoria's owner, J. J. Astor, who'd been lost on the *Titanic.*

The high-ceilinged lobby, with its crystal chandelier and dark walnut wainscoting, reminded Sam of the domed first-class lobby on the *Titanic,* with its grand staircase. Lush potted palms flanked marble pillars, and

French brocade chairs and settees were grouped on thick Persian carpets.

The doorman didn't want to let Star in, but the two dollars Jack slipped into the man's hand finally convinced him.

The lobby was crowded with reporters and photographers. There was even a newsreel camera and crew set up near the ballroom where the hearings were being held.

"Wait here a minute." Jack motioned Sam and Star to a vacant settee while he walked up to the front desk. Sam could see him asking questions, and he watched curiously as a reporter and photographer approached Jack. Sam supposed the press was so eager for news, they'd interview anybody.

A commotion on the other side of the room caught Sam's attention. The tall double doors of the ballroom opened, and reporters thronged forward, shouting questions. Flashbulbs popped as several people ducked out of the ballroom and headed for the elevators.

Sam heard someone shout: "Mr. Ismay, is it true . . ." but he didn't hear the rest of the question. He didn't need to. J. Bruce Ismay was here in this hotel, and at any moment, Star's rightful owner would see his dog and take him away.

Sam bent over Star, stroking him, memorizing him. Then he got down on his hands and knees on the lobby carpet and rested his head against Star's. The dog twisted around to crawl on Sam's lap, his hind legs sticking out awkwardly.

When Sam looked up again, he was staring at Mr. Ismay, with Jack at his elbow. The reporters had turned their attention to Senator William Smith, who was conducting the hearings. Ismay cast glances in both directions, but for the moment, there seemed to be no one else around.

"Yes, this *is* my dog," Ismay said, stretching his hand out to take Star's leash. Star burrowed his head under Sam's arm. Sam swallowed hard.

"I'm sorry about his tail, sir," Sam somehow managed to say. "It got caught in an oarlock on the lifeboat."

"Yes, well . . ." Ismay shrugged. "I'm sure it couldn't be helped. I don't know what to do with the dog until I can find him a kennel." He tugged pensively on one end of his waxed mustache, curling it around his finger.

"Come on, Star. Get up." Sam tried to lift the dog from his lap. Finally Star stood up, along with Sam, staying close to the boy's legs, tail tucked under and head low.

"Mr. Ismay?" A reporter had come out of nowhere

and stood with his notebook open, pencil poised. "Considering how many *people* didn't make it off the *Titanic*, it's practically a miracle that a dog survived, don't you think?"

Ismay looked startled.

A photographer appeared from behind a marble pillar and a flashbulb popped in Sam's face. As Sam tried to blink away the white spot in front of his eyes, he heard the reporter asking, "Is it true, Mr. Ismay, that this is *your* dog, a dog that was aboard the *Titanic*? Is it true, sir, that you managed to save your expensive show dog when over fifteen hundred human beings perished?"

Several other reporters had gathered around them, and Sam pulled Star closer.

Ismay backed up a step and put his hands up, as if he were trying to fend off the questions. He suddenly smiled, a strained smile, as if somebody were pinching him.

"*My* dog?" he blurted. "Preposterous! No, gentlemen, this isn't *my* dog at all. I have given this dog as a gift to the boy who saved him. It's the least I can do to mend one broken heart from all those who were lost on the *Titanic*. I, too, know how strange and lonely it feels to be a survivor."

The reporters crowded in around Ismay, although Sam could still see his face, towering over them all.

"You mean you didn't save the dog?" one reporter shouted.

"Of course not," Ismay said. "This boy did. That's why I'm giving him the dog. Though I'm afraid it's a small gesture in the face of so great a tragedy."

Jack took Sam by the elbow, leading him toward the lobby's doors. Star was right beside them.

"Mr. Ismay doesn't want Star?" Sam asked, not quite understanding—or believing—what had just happened.

"To be honest, Sam, it's probably just a public relations ploy for the president of the White Star Line, who certainly can't admit his whole ship went down but he didn't even lose his dog. Or maybe the man really does have a heart. Anybody can see that you and Star belong together."

Sam froze at the revolving doors and stared at Jack.

"So he's mine? Star's really mine?" he asked.

Jack nodded, and Sam burst into Bucky's familiar chorus: "Ta-ra-ra-boom-de-ay, If Star can really stay, It's gonna be okay, Ta-ra-ra-boom-de-ay."

"Well, let's go find your mother, pack our bags, take our dog, and go home," Jack said. "What do you say?"

"Yes," Sam agreed, meaning it more than he would have thought possible a week ago. A lifetime ago.

A flashbulb suddenly popped in his face, and Sam

blinked at a reporter who'd followed them out the door. "So, tell me," the man asked, "how did you save this dog when so many people were drowning all around you? Were you working for J. Bruce Ismay?"

"I never even *met* Mr. Ismay until today," Sam answered.

"So you saved the dog exactly how?" the reporter pressed.

"I didn't save him. Star saved me."

"Star is the dog's name, right?" The reporter scribbled frantically in his notebook. A photographer knelt and popped a flashbulb in Star's face. Star barked at the man and lunged forward on his lead. The photographer scuttled backward like a crab as more reporters joined the group. "Did you dress up in girls' clothing to sneak onto a lifeboat?" one of them called.

"No!" Sam knew he sounded angry. He *was* angry. He paused, and a grin spread across his face. "I dressed in my underwear."

Several reporters laughed. Jack squeezed Sam's shoulder and whispered, "Good for you!"

"Are you saying none of the officers shot at you to keep you out of the lifeboats? We heard there was shooting!" another reporter called.

"No! The officers didn't shoot at us! The officers

practically *threw* us into the lifeboats," Sam said. "They loaded people as fast as they could. They tried to put me on one, but I wouldn't let them."

"Why in the world wouldn't you want a lifeboat?" asked the reporter. "Weren't you afraid?"

Sam thought of Finn and the other ship's boys having a last smoke and not even trying to find a place in the crowded lifeboats. He thought about Bucky, standing bravely beside his father. He thought of Ann Isham, kneeling on the tilting deck with her arms around Toujours.

"Sure, I was scared," Sam said, staring down at Star. "Everybody was scared. But a lot of people, a lot of *my* friends, were really, really brave. I'll never forget that. But it all happened so fast. Do you understand?" Sam wanted to *make* them understand. "Nobody believed the *Titanic* could sink. All the newspapers called it 'unsinkable.' That's why none of the passengers believed the ship was sinking, right up until the last minute, until it was too late."

"Yes, but what about—"

"I think that's enough questions." Jack cut the reporter short. "The boy is tired. He's been through a lot and we have a ways to go to get home."

Jack looked down at Sam. Sam nodded. Pennsylvania had been his home once. It could be again.

Jack pushed open the lobby door and the sweet springtime scent of April in New York made Star bound forward onto the sidewalk, pulling Sam behind.

"Wait! You never told us," the reporter called. "*How* did you survive?"

The door was already closing.

Only Jack heard Sam's whispered answer.

"I got lucky. I followed my Star."

Map of *Titanic's* Voyage

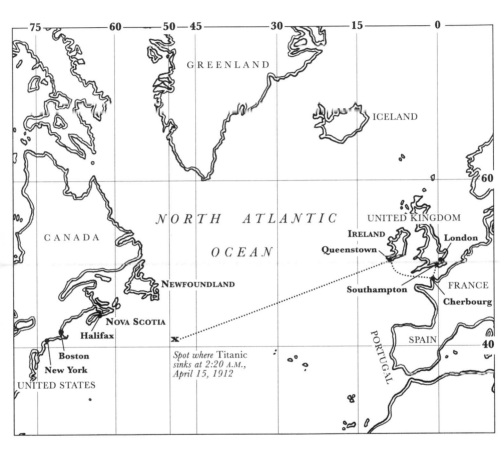

Time Line for *Titanic*

May 31, 1911

The *Titanic* is launched from the Belfast, Ireland, shipyard where it had been built.

Wednesday, April 10, 1912

7:30 A.M.   Passengers begin boarding in Southampton, England

12:00 P.M.   *Titanic* embarks on her maiden voyage

7:00 P.M.   *Titanic* arrives in Cherbourg, France

9:00 P.M.   *Titanic* leaves Cherbourg

Thursday, April 11, 1912

12:30 P.M.   The ship arrives in Queenstown (now Cobh), Ireland

2:00 P.M.   The ship leaves Queenstown for New York. There are 1,316 passengers and 891 crew members on board.

Thursday–Saturday, April 11–13, 1912

Titanic is at sea

Sunday, April 14, 1912

9:00 A.M.   *Titanic* receives its first telegraph warning of icebergs from the *Caronia*

1:42 P.M.   The ship receives the first of five more ice warnings from other ships

11:40 P.M.   *Titanic* strikes an iceberg

Monday, April 15, 1912

12:05 A.M. Lifeboats are uncovered and passengers are told
to put on life vests

12:15 A.M. First S.O.S. signal from *Titanic*

12:45 A.M. First distress rocket fired from *Titanic*

12:45 A.M. First lifeboat, Number 7, is lowered

1:40 A.M. Last distress rocket fired from *Titanic*

2:05 A.M. Last lifeboat, Collapsible D, is lowered. More
than 1,500 people are still on board.

2:10 A.M. Last wireless signal sent

2:20 A.M. *Titanic* sinks

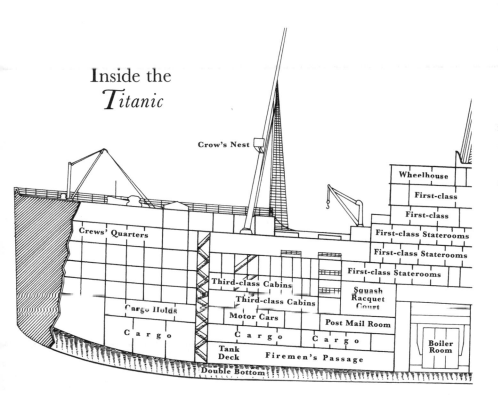

Inside the
Titanic

3:30 A.M.	Lifeboat passengers sight *Carpathia*'s rockets
4:10 A.M.	First lifeboat is picked up by *Carpathia*
8:30 A.M.	Last lifeboat is picked up by *Carpathia*
8:50 A.M.	*Carpathia* heads toward New York carrying an estimated 705 *Titanic* survivors

Thursday, April 18, 1912

| 8:00 P.M. | *Carpathia* arrives in New York harbor |

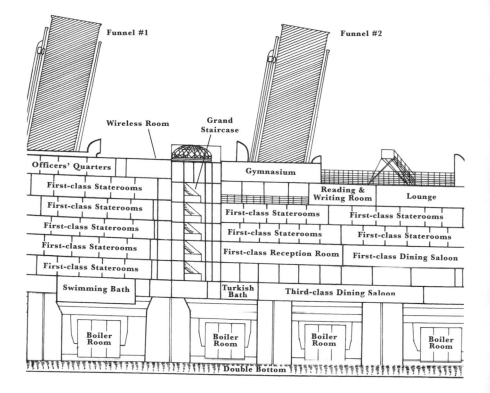

134

Fascinating Facts

The *Titanic* weighed 46,328 gross tons and was 882.5 feet long, 92.5 feet wide, and 175 feet tall from the bottom of its keel to the top of its funnels. In other words, it was eleven stories high and four city blocks long. It had two sets of four-cylinder engines that gave it a total of 50,000 horsepower. *Titanic* could travel 24 to 25 knots at full speed, approximately 28 miles per hour.

The *Titanic*'s "swimming bath" was 30 feet long and 6 feet deep at its deepest point. The "bath," which would be called a swimming pool

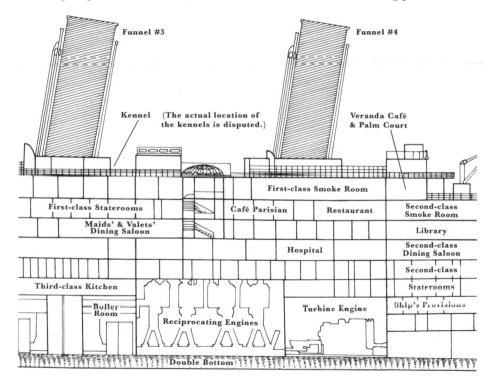

Funnel #3

Funnel #4

Kennel (The actual location of the kennels is disputed.)

Veranda Café & Palm Court

First-class Smoke Room

First-class Staterooms

Café Parisian

Restaurant

Second-class Smoke Room

Maids' & Valets' Dining Saloon

Library

Hospital

Second-class Dining Saloon

Second-class Staterooms

Third-class Kitchen

Boiler Room

Turbine Engine

Ship's Provisions

Reciprocating Engines

Double Bottom

today, was emptied and refilled daily with ocean water. Heated tiles lining the bath made the water warm. There were separate swimming hours for men and women and a small fee for using the bath.

The *Titanic* had forty-eight clocks, and all of them were controlled by a master clock in the Chart Room. As the *Titanic* moved across the Atlantic, its clocks changed by more than a half hour every day.

The first standard radio distress call was "CQD." In 1906 the International Radio Telegraphic Convention in Berlin created the signal "SOS" as a better way of calling for help. It was simple and easy to remember in Morse Code. Despite being formally designated as the

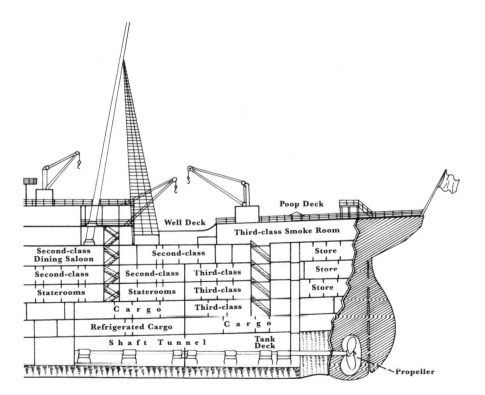

universal distress signal in 1908, "SOS" was not used until the night of *Titanic*'s sinking, when it was used for the very first time.

For nearly seventy-five years, the wreck of the *Titanic* lay undiscovered. Many explorers and researchers had tried to locate the wreck but had not been able to find it. In 1985 Dr. Robert D. Ballard and his team discovered the remains of *Titanic* resting 2½ miles below the Atlantic Ocean's surface. One year later, Dr. Ballard and two members of his team used a specially crafted submarine to photograph *Titanic*. These photographs were the first taken of the ship since its sinking.

Fascinating Mysteries

The Ship's Cat

Every ship sailing in 1912 had a ship's cat on board to kill vermin. Cats were also thought to bring ships good luck. According to the memoirs of *Titanic* stewardess Violet Constance Jessop in Titanic *Survivor: The Memoirs of Violet Jessop, Stewardess* (Sutton, 1997), there was a ship's cat that gave birth to a litter of four kittens during the ten days of travel between Belfast, Ireland, where *Titanic* was launched, and Southampton, England, where it took on its first passengers. But the cat reportedly carried her kittens off the ship as the passengers boarded on April 10. It was a very bad omen for *Titanic*'s maiden voyage. No one knows what prompted the cat to leave the ship.

The Wreck of the *Titan*

In 1898 Morgan Robertson's *The Wreck of the* Titan was published. It was a novel about the largest passenger ocean liner ever built, the *Titan*, which strikes an iceberg and sinks. Most of the passengers on board are lost, partly because of the insufficient number of lifeboats available. Although *The Wreck of the* Titan was published more than fourteen years before the sinking of the *Titanic*, the similarities between the novel and the events of April 14, 1912, led some people to believe that *The Wreck of the* Titan was an eerie premonition of the tragic events to come.

The Mummy's Curse

After *Titanic's* sinking, rumors of a mummy's curse causing the ship's ill fate spread widely. One survivor, Frederic Kimber Seward, remembered that a fellow passenger on board, William T. Stead, a journalist and spiritualist, had told him a story of the curse. Stead spoke of an Egyptian mummy case on board *Titanic* that, according to legend, brought bad luck, injury, and even death to anyone coming into contact with it. The curse supposedly caused the ship's sinking.

No evidence of a mummy was ever found among the *Titanic's* cargo. In fact, the "unlucky mummy case" had been presented to the British Museum in July 1889 and has been on public display ever since. It has only left the museum once, in 1990, when it was part of a temporary exhibition in Australia. The actual mummy to which the case belonged was left in Egypt.

Fascinating People

Samuel Harris and the dog Star, Lady Lavinia Cabot, Bucky Kingsbury and his parents, and Phineas MacDougal are fictional characters in this story. Everyone else was real. Approximately 1,500 lives were lost in the *Titanic* disaster, while only 700 people survived. As of October 2003, there were three Titanic survivors still living:

> Elizabeth Gladys Millvina Dean, Southampton, England
> Barbara Joyce West, Plymouth, England
> Lillian Gertrud Asplund, Shrewsbury, Massachusetts

SURVIVORS

Mr. and Mrs. Dickinson H. Bishop were returning to America from a honeymoon abroad when they boarded the *Titanic* with their little dog, Frou-Frou. The small white dog was left locked in its owners' cabin on B-deck on the night of *Titanic*'s sinking. Mr. and Mrs. Bishop both survived the sinking. While on Lifeboat Number 7, Mrs. Bishop recalled how an Egyptian fortune-teller had told her that she would survive a shipwreck and an earthquake before being killed in a car accident. She survived an earthquake on a later vacation in California and survived a serious car accident in 1913, but it left her with a fractured skull. She never fully recovered and died in 1916.

When Dr. Robert D. Ballard first looked into the B-deck portholes from his deep-ocean submersible, he imagined he could hear faint barking, the barking of Frou-Frou, still indignant over being left behind.

William Thornton Carter II (Willie Carter) was eleven years old when he boarded the *Titanic* with his mother, Lucile; father, William Ernest; and sister, Lucile. Mr. Carter saw his family safely to a lifeboat before himself taking a last-minute spot in Collapsible C, alongside J. Bruce Ismay. When young Willie and his mother and sister were boarding Lifeboat Number 4, boat chief Second

139

Steward George Dodd said no more boys would be allowed on board. Mrs. Carter placed a woman's hat on Willie's head, and the boy was permitted to board. The family left their two spaniels behind on the *Titanic*.

Robert Williams Daniel was a banker from Philadelphia, Pennsylvania, who survived the sinking of the ship. Some accounts state that he was rescued in Lifeboat Number 3; others say he jumped into the water and was saved by a passing lifeboat. His dog, Gamin de Pycombe, was seen dog-paddling through the frigid water during the sinking. Daniel met Mrs. Lucien P. Smith, a fellow *Titanic* survivor, while on board the *Carpathia*. They later married.

Colonel Archibald Gracie was a graduate of West Point Academy. His ancestors built Gracie Mansion in New York City, which in 1942 became the official residence of the city's mayor. Gracie had traveled to Europe on vacation and was returning on *Titanic*. Gracie was pulled under the water as the ship sank but managed to kick free of the undertow and swim to the overturned Collapsible B. While he survived the sinking, he died at home in New York in December 1912, having never fully recovered from that night.

Samuel Ernest Hemmings was a lamp trimmer on the *Titanic*. Hemmings was pulled out of the water after *Titanic*'s sinking by the survivors in Lifeboat Number 4.

Joseph Bruce Ismay was the son of Thomas Ismay, who was senior partner in the firm of Ismay, Imric and Company and founder of the White Star Line. In 1899 J. Bruce Ismay took over the business from his father. Ismay accompanied all his ships on their maiden voyages, including *Titanic*. He was rescued from the

Titanic in Collapsible C and was later criticized for living while so many other passengers died. Within a year of the sinking, he retired from the White Star Line and retreated into a very quiet life. In his later years, he would not allow anyone to speak the word *Titanic* in his presence.

Second Officer **Charles Lightoller** was in charge of loading the even-numbered lifeboats on the port side (left side) of *Titanic*. He only allowed women and children to board the lifeboats, not even allowing millionaire John Jacob Astor to join his pregnant wife when Astor asked to do so. After *Titanic* sank, Lightoller swam to overturned Collapsible A and took charge of keeping it afloat. He was *Titanic*'s senior surviving officer.

Walter John Perkis had served as an able-bodied seaman for sixteen years before transferring from the *Olympic* to the *Titanic* and taking on the position of quartermaster, a petty officer with navigational duties. He was put in command of Lifeboat Number 4 on the night of *Titanic*'s sinking and on June 5, 1912, took up his position on the *Olympic* once more.

Herbert John Pitman joined the White Star Line in 1906 and served as a junior officer on the *Dolphin, Majestic,* and *Oceanic* before becoming third officer on the *Titanic*. He managed the decks, supervised the quartermasters, and charted *Titanic*'s position by celestial navigation. On the night of the sinking, he was put in charge of Lifeboat Number 5.

VICTIMS

John Jacob Astor was a multimillionaire and was dubbed the world's richest man at the time of *Titanic*'s voyage. He was the owner of the Waldorf-Astoria Hotel in New York City. He boarded the *Titanic* with his pregnant, eighteen-year-old wife, Madeleine. Mr. Astor did not survive the sinking, but Madeleine did. Madeleine Astor claimed to have seen her husband on deck with their dog, an Airedale named Kitty, just before the ship broke apart. She returned to New York and gave birth to a son, whom she named after her husband.

Ann Elizabeth Isham had spent nine years abroad when she decided to return to the United States to spend the summer months with her brother. She was one of only four women in first class to die in the *Titanic* disaster. Some *Titanic* experts suggested that Isham brought a large dog, possibly a Great Dane or a Saint Bernard, onto the ship with her and that she later refused to board a lifeboat without her dog. A few days after *Titanic*'s sinking, the German passenger liner *Bremen,* passing through the debris, reported seeing a woman, floating lifeless in the water, with her arms around a large dog.

First Officer **William Murdoch** was in charge of loading the odd-numbered lifeboats on the starboard (right) side of the ship. He allowed men to board lifeboats as well as women and children. He was the officer in charge of the bridge when *Titanic* struck the iceberg. His body was never recovered from the wreckage.

Captain Edward John Smith began his career as a seaman at the age of thirteen and joined White Star Line in 1880. He gained his first command in 1887 and subsequently commanded the *Republic, Coptic, Majestic, Baltic, Adriatic,* and *Olympic.* He was planning to retire but accepted the honor of taking the *Titanic* on her maiden voyage in 1912 on what was supposed to be his final command. As the lore of the sea tells us a good captain should, Captain Smith went down with the ship.

Ida and Isidor Straus owned Macy's department store in New York City. As *Titanic* began to sink, Ida refused to leave her husband and gave her seat on a lifeboat to a younger passenger. Ida and Isidor died together.

Decks of the $Titanic$

(BO) Boat Deck: *Where the lifeboats and the kennels are located*
(A) Promenade Deck
(B) Bridge Deck: *Where Sam's room is*
(C) Shelter Deck
(D) Saloon Deck: *Where Sam eats in the dining room*

(E) Upper Deck
(F) Middle Deck
(G) Lower Deck: *Where Sam and Bucky swim in the swimming bath*
(O) Orlop Deck: *Where Sam and Bucky hide in the boiler rooms*
(S) Sun Deck

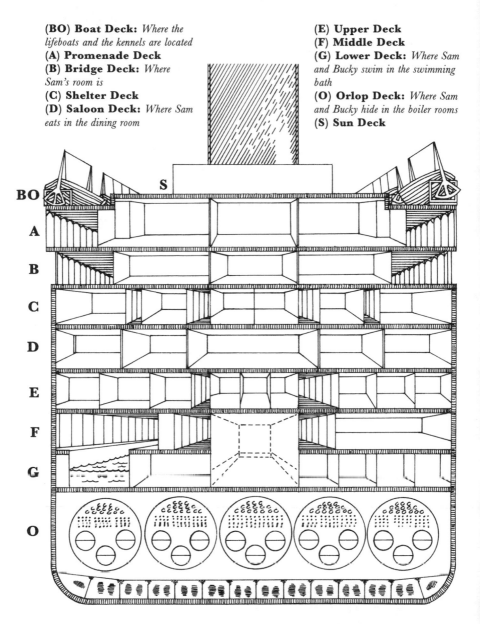

144

Recommended Reading for Young People

(F) = fiction, (NF) = nonfiction

Adams, Simon. *Eyewitness Books:* Titanic. New York: DK Inc., 1999. (NF)

Ballard, Robert D. *Finding the* Titanic. New York: Scholastic Inc., 1993. (NF)

Bunting, Eve. *SOS* Titanic. New York: Harcourt Brace, 1996. (F)

Corning, Daisy, and Stone Spedden. *Polar, the* Titanic *Bear.* Toronto, Ontario, Canada: Madison Press Books, 1994. (F)

Donnelly, Judy. *The* Titanic *Lost . . . and Found.* New York: Random House, 1987. (NF)

Giuliano, Geoffrey. *That Fateful Night: True Stories of* Titanic *Survivors—In Their Own Words!* (audiobook). New York: Bantam Doubleday Dell Audio Publishing, 1998. (NF)

Gormley, Beatrice. *Back to the* Titanic! Travelers Through Time series. New York: Scholastic Inc., 1994. (F)

Lawlor, Laurie. *1912: A* Titanic *Journey Across the Sea.* American Sister series. New York: Simon & Schuster, 1998. (F)

Lord, Walter. *A Night to Remember.* New York: Holt, 1955. (NF)

———. *The Night Lives On.* New York: Bantam Books, 1976. (NF)

Lynch, Don. Titanic: *An Illustrated History.* New York: Hyperion, 1992. (NF)

National Geographic. *Secrets of the* Titanic (video). Washington, D.C.: National Geographic Society, 1986. (NF)

Osborne, Mary Pope. *Tonight on the* Titanic. Magic Tree House series. New York: Random House, 1999. (F)

Tanaka, Shelley. *On Board the* Titanic. New York: Hyperion, 1996. (NF)

White, Ellen Emerson. *Voyage on the Great* Titanic*: The Diary of Margaret Ann Brady.* Dear America series. New York: Scholastic Inc., 1998. (F)

Williams, Barbara. Titanic *Crossing.* New York: Scholastic Inc., 1995. (F)

Source Notes

My primary sources included *Titanic* expert George Behe (thanks, George!); the late *Titanic* legend Walter Lord (whom I was privileged to visit); *Titanic* survivor Elizabeth Gladys "Millvina" Dean (whom I was privileged to meet at the 35th Anniversary of the *Titanic* Historical Society). The *Titanic* Historical Society publishes *The Titanic Commutator* quarterly. I was also lucky enough to visit the Society's museum in Indian Orchard, Massachusetts; the maritime museum in Southampton, England; the maritime museum in Los Angeles, California, with its huge model of the *Titanic;* and special *Titanic* exhibitions on the *Queen Mary* in Long Beach, California, in Orlando, Florida, and exhibitions in Atlantic City, New Jersey, and in Newport News, Virginia.

Several books from the recommended reading list for young people also provided valuable source material, especially Don Lynch's Titanic*: An Illustrated History,* Walter Lord's *A Night to Remember* and *The Night Lives On,* and Geoffrey Giuliano's *That Fateful Night: True Stories of* Titanic *Survivors—In Their Own Words!* Don Lynch and George Behe are the preeminent U.S. *Titanic* scholars at present, and Ken Marschall (who illustrated Titanic*: An Illustrated History* and many other *Titanic* books) is the definitive *Titanic* illustrator. On the other side of the pond, Eaton & Hass would doubtless be considered the preeminent *Titanic* scholars.

Adams, Simon. *Eyewitness Books:* Titanic. New York: DK Inc., 1999.

Archbold, Rick, and Dana McCauley. *Last Dinner on the* Titanic. New York: Hyperion, 1997.

Ballard, Robert D. *The Disaster of the* Titanic. New York: Time Warner, 1987.

———. "Epilogue for *Titanic.*" *National Geographic,* October 1987.

———. "How We Found *Titanic.*" *National Geographic,* December 1985.

———. "A Long Last Look at *Titanic.*" *National Geographic,* December 1986.

Ballard, Robert D., and Rick Archbold. *Lost Liners.* New York: Hyperion, 1997.

Behe, George. Titanic: *Safety, Speed and Sacrifice.* Polo, Ill.: Transportation Trails, 1997.

Biel, Steven. *Down with the Old Canoe: A Cultural History of the* Titanic *Disaster.* London: W. W. Norton & Co., 1996.

———. *Titanica: The Disaster of the Century in Poetry, Song, and Prose.* London: W. W. Norton & Co., 1998.

Bryceson, Dave. *The* Titanic *Disaster: As reported in the British National Press, April–July 1912.* London: W. W. Norton & Co., 1997.

Butler, Daniel Allen. *Unsinkable: The Full Story.* Mechanicsburg, Pa.: Stackpole Books, 1998.

Eaton, John, and Charles Hass. Titanic*: A Journey Through Time.* London: W. W. Norton & Co., 1999.

———. Titanic: *Triumph and Tragedy* (second edition). London: W. W. Norton & Co., 1994.

Garrison, Webb. *Treasury of* Titanic *Tales.* Nashville, Tenn.: Rutledge Hill Press, 1998.

Gillespie, John and Vera. *The* Titanic *Man: Carlos F. Hurd.* Grover, Mo.: Vera & John Gillespie, 1996.

Gracic, Colonel Archibald. Titanic: *A Survivor's Story.* Chicago: Academy Chicago Publishers, 1998. (First published as *The Truth About the* Titanic in 1913.) *(survivor)*

Hirshberg, Charles. "The Tragedy of the *Titanic.*" *Life,* June 1997.

Hyslop, Donald, Alastair Forsyth, and Sheila Jemima. Titanic *Voices*. New York: St. Martin's Press, 1997.

Jessop, Violet. *Titanic Survivor*. Dobbs Ferry, N.Y.: Sheridan House, Inc., 1997. (Published long after the author's death.)

Kent, Deborah. *The* Titanic. Cornerstones of Freedom series. Danbury, Conn.: Grolier Publishing, 1994.

Louden-Brown, Paul. *The White Star Line: An Illustrated History 1869 1934*. Norfolk, England: Ship Pictorial Publications, 1991.

MacInnis, Joseph. "*Titanic:* Tragedy in Three Dimensions." *National Geographic,* August 1998.

Marriott, Leo. Titanic. New York: Smithmark Publishers Inc., 1997.

Marshall, Logan. *The Sinking of the* Titanic. Edited by Bruce Caplan. Seattle, Wash.: Hara Publishing, 1997.

McMillan, Beverly, Lehrer Stanley, and the staff of the Mariners Museum, Newport News, Va. Titanic, *Fortune & Fate.* New York: Simon & Schuster, 1998.

O'Donnell, E. E. *The Last Days of the* Titanic. Dublin, Ireland: Wolfhound Press, 1997.

Quinn, Paul J. Titanic *at Two.* Saco, Maine: Fantail Press, 1997.

Thayer, John B. *The Sinking of the S.S.* Titanic. Chicago: Academy Chicago Publishers, 1998. (First published in 1940.) *(survivor)*

Tibballs, Geoff. *The* Titanic. Pleasantville, N.Y.: Reader's Digest, 1997.

Wade, Wyn Craig. *The* Titanic: *End of a Dream.* New York: Penguin Books, 1979.

Wels, Susan. Titanic: *Legacy of the World's Greatest Ocean Liner.* New York: Time Life Books and The Discovery Channel, 1997.

Winocour, Jack, editor. *The Story of the* Titanic *as Told by Its Survivors.* New York: Dover Publications, 1960. This book reprints *The*

Loss of the S.S. Titanic by Lawrence Beesley, 1912; *The Truth About the* Titanic by Archibald Gracie, 1913; Titanic *and Other Ships,* by Commander Charles Lightoller, 1935; and *Thrilling Tale by* Titanic*'s Surviving Wireless Man,* by Harold Bride, 1912 *(all survivors).*

And finally, it would be unfair not to mention James Cameron's famous 1997 Academy Award–winning film, *Titanic,* which infected the world (including me) with *Titanic* fever all over again.